# The Castle Of Troubled Souls Hotel

DREW BARLOWE

Published by Drew Barlowe
Publishing partner: Paragon Publishing, Rothersthorpe
First published 2023

ISBN 978-1-78792-026-2

Book design, layout and production management by Into Print
www.intoprint.net
+44 (0)1604 832149

# 1

**S**he turned up suddenly, out of the blue. There were quite a few guests staying at the Castle Hotel that day and she simply booked one of the rooms. Richard was dead. She must have realised that. Nobody let her know about the funeral then because nobody knew where she had gone.

The receptionist was new and took no notice of her name when booking and Joann was surprised to see her in the hotel foyer. She found it rather funny that Louise had appeared so unexpectedly after ten years and she wondered what she might want.

Louise looked good, radiant with a charming smile and blonde, curly hair around her pretty face. She must have been thirty now, but she attracted more attention than when she was younger. She looked fit, had carefully selected clothes, maturity added to her beauty.

Their parting ten years ago was not a pleasant one and Joann wasn't sure what to expect from her.

Richard and Louise had been secretly dating because his mother didn't approve. When the romance came to light, she forbade him from seeing her and Louise left town in despair.

He never married. Soon after she left he developed a heart disease and passed away two years later.

"I found out only recently," Louise said and it seemed that she was sad for a moment, but after a while she raised her head and looked at Joann with large, pale blue eyes. Joann stood silently as the memories of her brother overwhelmed her. She was still confused by Louise's sudden visit and was not ready to talk to her right now.

"I am staying only for one night. I'm picking up the keys to my cottage tomorrow morning." She seemed cordial and wanting to start a conversation, but hesitated when she saw that Joann didn't trust her.

"Well, enjoy your stay. Let me know if you need anything," Joann replied and left to return to her duties, leaving Louise alone in the hotel foyer.

Louise looked around, amazed. Time had changed nothing here and everything looked just like years ago. Impressive stone arches resting on decorative columns, stairs with carved wooden handrails and dark red carpet. In the corner, between the stairs and the corridor leading to the hotel bar, there was a suit of armour, polished and shiny. In the opposite corner was a bronze bust of Shakespeare and a stone sculpture of a young woman by the wall leading to the hotel parlour. The high ceiling was adorned with the same large crystal chandelier she remembered.

For a moment, Louise was under the illusion that it had not been ten years since she'd left. That she'd been here only yesterday and, as usual, she was waiting for Richard to join her. The impression was so strong that she thought she would see him in a minute, walking down the corridor towards her, smiling, in a white shirt with rolled up sleeves, and they would leave together chatting and laughing. It seemed to her that she could hear his happy laugh and approaching steps. She waited in tension, but the man didn't come and the return to reality hurt more than she expected.

* * *

Joann entered the office. It was a spacious, comfortable room with two attached desks in the middle and one against the wall. A leather sofa was by the window with a small coffee table. She sat down at her desk, rested her elbows on the surface, and placed her chin on her interlaced fingers. The unexpected arrival of Louise brought back painful memories of her sick, dying brother and aroused strange emotions. She still had Richard before her eyes and remembered the day of their parting. She saw him and Louise together, standing there at the bottom of the white cliffs. The wind was blowing from the sea and it combed her curly hair and his white shirt was fluttering. He was kissing her hands desperately, cradling them tenderly to his face, and tears were running down her cheeks. It looked, for some reason, like it was no longer appropriate for him to hug her or kiss her lips. As if her hands were the only part of her he allowed himself to hold and cherish for the last time. Joann pulled back and ran away before they could notice her presence.

She had been about fifteen at the time and this scene saddened her, but she knew from her mother that they were not supposed to be together and she understood that all this was wrong and that Louise was bad and this is why she should not feel sorry for what she saw. Joann felt a strange surge of sorrow and covered her face with her hands. She sat motionless, in silence with her memories, delving into the past.

There was a knock and the door opened slightly. Alfred's head appeared first. He looked around to make sure he didn't disturb and then entered the room. She lowered her hands and looked at him, slowly returning to the present.

"There's a handyman here looking for a job, and since we lost Tom I thought…"

"Right, let him in," she said, shaking off depressing thoughts.

Alfred beckoned to someone, and another man entered the office. He wore shabby clothes, and was holding a cup. He had dark hair and his face was devastated by the sun, making him look older than he probably was. She thought he couldn't be more than thirty-eight or forty years old.

"I'm Ben, Ben Smith," he introduced himself. She found that he had a rather common appearance and it seemed to her that he felt a little insecure.

"Are you local, Ben?" she asked him.

"I am from the next village," he replied, staring at her as if her face seemed familiar to him.

"Do you know building and refurbishment work?"

"I have been a builder all my life, I can do anything," he said with great confidence.

"That's good because our handyman retired and went fishing. We had a leak a few days ago and it flooded one bedroom. I'll show you."

She led him upstairs and down a narrow corridor with deep red carpets and small iron windows on the left-hand side. Large, old paintings in gold and dark walnut frames hung on the walls between sconces in brass with frosted bell-shaped glass. She opened one of the heavy, arched doors on the right side of the corridor and showed him the room. It was quite large, with a four-poster bed in the middle and a white French-style dressing table by the window. A big stain was very much visible on the ceiling and two walls. They'd need to be painted and the wallpaper redone. In the bathroom upstairs, the linoleum had to be replaced, the wall on which the pipe had cracked re-painted, and a few other jobs.

Ben said that it would take him a few days and she was pleased with that. They went down to the office and she gave him a little advance from the money box and they agreed she would pay him the rest when the job was done. Joann felt relieved; she had two weddings coming up and the rooms were already booked and paid for.

It was half-past four when Joann closed the office and went to the hotel bar to see if there were any familiar faces. A few people were already there. The giant fireplace had been lit because, even though it was just the beginning of September, the day turned out to be rainy and the temperature had dropped significantly. The fire burned brightly, spreading cosiness. One couple was sitting at a table by the fireplace with glasses of wine. Jack, the bartender, was serving scotch whiskey to a man at the bar. She gave him a quick look. His shirt was an impeccable white and his appearance was good. She smiled at him and he smiled back.

Edgar was sitting at the small, wooden table in the corner. She had known him for years. Their parents were very good friends and often joked that they would marry him and Joann off when they grew up. She once imagined they would be together, but something had changed over time and they just remained friends. His family owned a golf club and an indoor bowling club and were doing very well. He noticed her and waved. She came up to him and sat at his table.

"I just popped in to get a drink," he said, but it looked to her like he'd had one or two already. He was a strong, well-built man and very direct. "What will you drink?" he asked, looking straight at her. "Gin and tonic?"

"Nothing, thanks. Not today. I'm going home earlier, my mother wasn't feeling well last night," she replied, genuinely concerned about her mother who had been suffering from severe depression and anxiety for years.

"Get her a nurse to keep her company," he said roughly, then lit a cigarette and drank some whiskey.

There was Shirley who cleaned the house three times a week, and Mildred the cook who came for a couple of hours each day to help with meals, but nobody who would come every day and keep her company. She wasn't sure if her mother would accept a full-time nurse, but she would enquire around.

"I'm only checking everything is in order here before I leave," she said, looking around discreetly. A few more people came in and stood at the bar.

"Everything is fine here the old man knows his job." He looked at the young bartender and winked to him but got no response as Jack was busy serving drinks to the guests who had just arrived.

"How's business?" she asked him.

"Everything's great." He smiled with satisfaction and straightened his back. "Actually, I'm planning to take a little vacation somewhere exotic. "Do you fancy going with me?" he asked with a note of intimacy in his voice.

"Me? Don't joke." She was surprised by this offer and looked at him coldly. Friendship was the only feeling she had for him and she thought he realised that.

"I'm not joking, Jo, I am dead serious," he said loudly, clearly irritated by her cold reaction.

"We are only friends," she said.

"We could be more than that, you know." He leaned close to her.

"I prefer it as it is. Let's just be friends," she said firmly.

A tall, slim woman entered the bar. She noticed Edgar and came over to him. Joann recognised her as the milk-man's daughter, Lucy.

"Can I speak to you for a minute?" she asked him, and Joann sensed the nervousness in her voice. She was about twenty, had blue-grey eyes and blonde hair falling over her shoulders and Joann thought that it was lacking a proper hairdo.

"I'm busy now," he said glumly looking down at his drink. "I'll come and speak to you later, Lucy."

"That's okay." Joann looked at her friendly. "I was just leaving," she said. She stood up and turned towards the door. Edgar stood up too, finished his drink in one sip and followed her out.

The narrow corridor leading to the main hall was empty. The stone walls rounded in the shape of an arch creating the impression of tunnel, a faint light illuminated the old framed maps hanging on the walls. He caught up with her and they stopped.

"I have been waiting for you for a long time, Jo," he said reproachfully.

"Waiting?" Joann was indignant. "What about that blonde, blue-eyed girl and a couple of others before her?" She put her hands on her hips in a fighting stance. She couldn't believe he was offering her a relationship while probably still having an affair with that girl. She always knew he was impudent, but this time he'd crossed the line.

"It's because you're always cold towards me," he tried to explain calmly. "Yes, I had an affair or two but it meant nothing."

"But it put me off." She turned away from him.

He grabbed her arm and touched her hair with his face. "All I want from you is to give us a chance." He drew her closer to himself.

"It hurts, Edgar!" She pulled her arm out of his grip, ignored him and started towards the main exit. His face grew red with anger.

"If you think I'll just let you go, you are bloody wrong," he shouted with anger and shook his hand, his finger pointing at her while she walked away.

# 2

lfred drove her home with the business car. He was a nice man in his late forties. He was the hotel porter and sometimes chauffeured guests from the station to the hotel and back. The afternoon was dark and rainy. After a few minutes of driving, they turned onto an alley of trees and at its end was a large Georgian house. It boasted wonderful symmetry and perfect proportions. The imposing front door was flanked by white columns and had a beautiful panelled window design above the opening. There were four long windows on each side of the door with decorative brick headers, and a gravel path leading up to it. The house had three reception rooms and ten bedrooms, and was sitting on two hectares of land. Joann adored it and couldn't imagine living elsewhere, although it seemed to be too big for their needs. After her father died, and later her brother, only Joann and her mother lived there with two dogs, a black Gordon Setter and a lemon-and-white Pointer. She always thought that when she started her own family, they would live in this house. Though time passed, it didn't happen, and she was still single.

Alfred left her in front of the house and drove back.

"One day this house will be full of children and people," she said, walking inside.

She found her mother in the kitchen making tea. She liked the homely feel of the kitchen. The round table stood in the centre and a large chalk-coloured, glass-fronted dresser was against the wall opposite the front door, displaying crockery and silverware. The copper sink and cupboard handles matched the brick mantel over the stove, the marble worktop and the red ceramic floor tiles. Large sash double windows looked out over the garden, captivating with simplicity and the symmetry of greenery.

"I heard a car and thought to make tea." Her mother looked pleased and Joann was glad to find her in a good mood. She was in her late sixties, of medium height. Around her neck was an emerald pendant that she always wore in memory of her late husband. The slightly hunched figure revealed that she was in poor health. She brought a cake stand from the pantry, put it on the table and cut two pieces.

"How are you feeling today, Mum?" Joann sat down at the round table.

"I am very well. I went on a walk, popped in to the castle and stayed for lunch." She put the pieces of cake on two plates.

"Why didn't you come to the office and say hello?"

"I did but you were apparently busy somewhere else."

"Did Alfred drive you back home?"

"No, why should he? The weather was fine then and it felt good to walk back," she answered. "Don't you worry about me. I'm still holding up pretty well."

The kettle boiled. She poured water into the teapot, set it

on the table with two cups and sat across from Joann.

"You know what, they told me that horrible woman Louise came back. Is it true?" she asked, a little agitated. Louise's name had not been mentioned in this house for years and Joann was subconsciously afraid of talking about her. It happened only once, at the cemetery, when they were putting flowers on Richard's and her father's graves when she suddenly said she was curious what Louise was doing now.

"Well, I think so, yes," she answered. She took the teapot and, avoiding her mother's eyes, poured the tea.

"This is absurd. What can she want from us now?" She poured milk into a cup and stirred a teaspoon nervously. Although many years passed it was obvious that she still had deep-seated feelings of hatred and resentment towards that woman.

"I don't think she wants anything, Mum." Joann tried to stay calm but inside, her nervousness was starting to grow.

"So why did she come back? Why was she in the Castle?" She was getting more agitated. "I know what she wants. She wants revenge. Because I forbade her from marrying my son, but I had to. She wasn't the right sort for him. She came from nowhere and was nobody, just a poor orphan, and yet she seduced him by her beauty, twisted him round her little finger. He was ready to marry her and wanted my blessing. I couldn't allow it. Now she wants to make people hate us. She wants to ruin us. They always come back for revenge."

She was visibly upset and Joann wasn't sure how to calm her down. She only stared at her with wide, sad eyes.

"Nonsense, I really doubt it, Mum. She's just visiting," she tried to reassure her.

"Why didn't she come back when Richard was dying?" she asked and Joann sensed a clear resentment in her voice.

"She didn't know. She only found out recently that he passed away."

"You spoke to her?!"

"Yes, briefly."

"He died for her." Her voice broke and she started to sob. She took out a little handkerchief and blew her nose, then pressed the emerald pendant to her chest.

"Mum, please. Richard had a weak heart. No one knew about it until he got sick. The doctor said he might have had it for years without realising."

"My dear boy was dying of love for her and she wasn't there. Why didn't she come back to save him? Why didn't she…?" She covered her face with her hands and sobbed loudly. Joann walked over and embraced her.

"It's alright, Mum. It's alright now," she repeated, gently. After a while she stopped sobbing and rested her head on Jo's shoulder.

The telephone rang in the hall. Joann went to pick it up and talked for a while.

"Who was it?" her mother asked.

"The Greenbergs. They want me in the office at nine o'clock tomorrow."

"They found out about her return."

"It's just business as usual, Mum," Joann said, trying not to go back to that topic. She sat down at the table and poured another cup of tea.

"Edgar phoned again today. He said he'd been trying to get hold of you for the last few days. It looks to me like you're avoiding him. Why are you tormenting this poor man?" she asked with slight reproach.

"I talked to him already. Today," said Joann.

"I am glad you did. He is so nice and such a gentleman, you know. I think he is serious about you and I am so pleased for you." She put her small, wrinkled hand on top of Joann's palm and Joann gently put her hand on top. The frail, sick woman was all she had and she held on to her.

# 3

The Greenbergs were her business partners. They were nice people but relations between them were not excellent. Joann put the blame on the age gap as they were in their fifties and she was twenty-five. They had one son, Julius, who had travelled for most of his life, but five years ago settled in America.

The Greenbergs had been on a trip to London for a couple of days and she had run the hotel rather well without them. She wondered what they might want to talk to her about, but she doubted that it would be something exciting.

Cecilia Greenberg was a dark-haired, plump woman. She wore dark red lipstick and strong white gardenia perfume. She had on an ankle-length dress and low-heeled shoes. Her large, leather purse sat on the desk. Cecilia walked over to Joann to say hello and kissed her very gently on the cheek. Her husband Hugh was short and greyish. He wore a grey suit with double-breasted lapels and tapered trousers. He leaned his back against the desk, slightly sitting on the counter.

"How was London?" Joann asked them, sitting on the sofa by the window. She was glad to see them, but she felt some tension in their demeanour.

"Wonderful," answered Cecilia, walking nervously around the room.

"But we are glad to be back home," said Hugh, and he confirmed it with a big smile.

"How were things here?" Cecilia asked, taking another look round around the room.

"We heard that Louise came back," Hugh said.

"Yes, she did," Joann answered, waiting for their reaction.

"That's a trouble," he added.

"She seems to be friendly, but I don't know what to make of it," said Joann.

"Oh, that's rather obvious, my dear," said Cecilia, stopping and turning towards her. "She wants money, of course. She can give you a bad name and if the gossip spreads it might ruin the business."

"That's a trouble," Hugh repeated.

"If I were you," she continued, "I would try to reach some sort of agreement with her."

"What do you mean if you were me?" Joann asked. "Aren't we all together in this? We are partners. Aren't we?"

"Well, not exactly," answered Cecilia. "Not anymore." She was silent for a moment and continued, "We decided to sell our hotel shares."

"What?!" Joann stood up and took a few nervous steps around the room.

"We had to," said Hugh.

"Well, yes. You see, my child," said Cecilia, "we made some investments and put our money in risky business."

"Risky business?!" Joann repeated, terrified. "My God. What did you do?"

"There's no need to go into details about it now," she answered. "It's all behind us now, thank God, but we had to sell our hotel shares immediately to cover debts."

"Julius advised us," Hugh added.

"Yes," said Cecilia. "Julius told us to sell the shares and move with him to Bermuda. His business there is doing very well." She searched for something in her purse and took out a golden compact. She looked in the small mirror and, with a few movements, powdered her face.

"This is terrible. I feel very sorry for you. But why didn't you say anything before?" Joann asked. "There was no advertisement in the local press either."

"We didn't go local," Hugh answered. "Julius advised us not to."

"Yes," Cecilia continued. "We gave the advert directly to London, to find somebody with money, who could pay decently with cash." She took a few steps around the room.

"Why didn't you ask me?" asked Joann. "Don't I have right to pre-emption?"

"To be honest, Jo," answered Cecilia, turning towards her again, "you wouldn't be able to get such an amount of money. Your mother's house and your part of the hotel are still on a huge mortgage because your father wasn't insured when he passed away. You can't even afford full-time home service anymore."

That was true and she couldn't argue. In the summer, the hotel was usually full of guests and brought a good return, but some winter months were very quiet and then she had to pay back both mortgages from the savings.

"This is a complete shock to me." Joann thought for a

moment that this wasn't really happening.

"Don't be hysterical, my dear," said Cecilia. "I can understand how you must feel, of course, but try to understand our feelings too. It was a very difficult decision to make. Besides, it's only your business partner that changes. Everything else remains as normal as ever. You will still have your forty-five percent of the shares."

Joann fell into temporary retreat. She had known the Greenbergs since she was little and had worked with them for years. She was not prepared for such a huge, unexpected change and was already starting to worry about her relationship with the new shareholders.

"Who is the new partner?" she asked after a while.

"Mr Garrett Fereday," said Cecilia. "He was here this morning at seven o'clock," she stressed. "When you were still sleeping tightly in your bed."

"Ha, ha, ha," Hugh laughed out loud.

"He had a look around and said he didn't need time to make up his mind and he was happy to sign straight away," she continued. "There are only some formalities left. Oh, yes, and he wants to meet you at lunchtime to discuss some ideas of his."

Joann instinctively looked in to the large, silver-framed mirror hanging on the wall. The first thing she thought about was her appearance as she wanted to make a good impression on the new partner. She was a slim brunette with hazel eyes adorned with gold and brown eyeshadow and straight eyebrows. Her nicely proportioned lips were painted a rose burgundy and her long, slightly wavy hair was pinned up with black pearl hairpins. She was wearing a light silk blouse with ornamental tie and long puffed sleeves with long cuffs and dark, wide-leg trousers. She thought, regretfully, that a dress or a suit would make her look more feminine.

"We don't want any ceremonial farewell," said Cecilia as she hung her bag over her shoulder.

"We wouldn't be able to bear it," Hugh said, looking at her, and she saw the sadness in his eyes. "We will spend the rest of our lives in Bermuda."

"Yes," said Cecilia. "Julius announced his engagement and we are hoping to have grandchildren in the near future. Well, there is nothing else left but to wish you good luck, and remember to keep in touch, Jo. We'll pop in to say goodbye to your dearest mother of course."

She walked over to Joann and gave her the same gentle kiss on the cheek.

"We will miss you terribly," said Joann.

Hugh had tears in his eyes. "We spent such a long time here." He sobbed quietly as he hugged her and Joann patted him on the shoulder for encouragement. They went out the back door, straight into the parking lot and got into their car. Joann stood alone in the middle of the large room.

\* \* \*

Garrett Fereday was about thirty-five. He was of average height with dark-blond hair combed to one side. He wore brown trousers and a slightly lighter checked jacket that gave him quite a local look. Not as she imagined a London businessman would be, in a dark, perfectly cut suit. There was something untidy about the way he'd tied his tie, as if he didn't care about such mundane details, and his face was devoid of severity. The warm, friendly smile he welcomed her with fit perfectly to his image, which surprised her entirely.

He invited her to lunch and she accepted. They sat in the Castle restaurant, in a private part, separated from the main room by a beautiful stained-glass wall. She ordered crispy fried calamari with garnish for starter, and a roast duck crown with turnip, peach and a red wine sauce for main course, and he took the same. That was the hotel's speciality. She expected him to try the menu. She was proud of it and trusted the chefs, hoping they would put even more effort into the preparation of this meal to satisfy her guest.

The waiter served the starter and they began to eat. The main hall in the restaurant was slowly filling up with people coming for a hot lunch. There were muffled sounds of conversations and the clatter of cutlery.

"I roughly checked the accounting books," Garrett said, "and they seem okay." He stopped and looked at her, waiting for her reaction but she showed no emotions.

"I had a good look around too. I think we should rebuild the big tower. That would give us two more rooms." He spoke without haste but there was an enthusiasm in his voice. "The small tower and dungeon after adaptation could be open for visitors." He fell silent, still waiting for her to answer and looked at her curiously.

Joann was far from sharing his enthusiasm. She couldn't believe how quickly he took matters into his own hands and it irritated her. Especially that he was not the first one to come up with these ideas. They had such plans before, but there never seemed to be enough money left to do it and she wondered how he thought they would pay for it.

He spotted her irritation and smiled. "Something to think about," he said, then he cut a piece of garnish and put it in his mouth.

"I agree, it sounds like a good plan," she replied coldly and settled herself more comfortably on the chair. She watched him closely and discreetly. The way he spoke and moved drew in her mind an image of a man of cooperation upon whom it would depend for the future success of her business. She remembered now seeing his name in the newspaper in connection with the opening of some factory. He came from old family money and had powerful friends. She thought she had to be careful with him.

"Have you ever thought about changing the name of the hotel?" he asked.

"No, I haven't. Not even once. I've been used to this name since childhood. The name *The Castle of Troubled Souls Hotel*' has been attracting customers alright for years now," she answered, a little surprised that he doubted the name.

"I was thinking more of something like The Excalibur Hotel." He looked at her inquiringly.

"Nice. Or The Morning Mist Castle or The Evening Mist Castle," she suggested, picking up on his train of thought.

He didn't comment but stared at her for a moment in silence as if he wanted to guess the personality of the woman sitting in front of him. The waiter served the main course.

"This looks delicious," he said and she thought it was nice of him to comment, although she was convinced that he would want to make changes to the menu as well. They started to eat and fell silent for a while.

"Tell me something about yourself, Jo. You are very young. You have lots of responsibilities on your shoulders."

"Well, I'm alright," she started, swallowing a morsel of meat. It was obvious to her that they had to find out something about each other. "My parents married late. My father bought this hotel together with the Greenbergs when I was little. He died in a car accident eleven years ago, and my older brother three years later from heart disease. My mother couldn't recover from those painful happenings and failed in health. She's already in her late sixties and I'm worried about her. I was only seventeen when I took it over and managed the hotel together with the Greenbergs."

"You have no other family?" he asked. He was looking at her with a warm, benevolent look that made her feel quite relaxed.

"No, my mother was the only child. There was an uncle and his wife from my father's side but they both died childless. They left all their money for dogs' charities." She took a sip of wine and thought that it tasted excellent. She noticed that he didn't drink much, his glass was almost full still.

"You have no fiancé?" he asked directly.

"No, there isn't any."

"Now you've surprised me." He smiled again.

"What about you?" she asked. She was very curious about how much he would reveal. "Are you married? Do you have children?"

"No, I am not. There is nothing interesting about my life, I am afraid," he started, like a man who doesn't want to talk too much about himself. "Business has been the only thing in my life since I can remember. My father taught me this when

I was a boy." He looked at her and must have read from the expression on her face that this answer was not sufficient. "There was someone," he added. "Meredith." Uttering this name, he thought deeply, as if he'd stepped back into a past unknown to her, and his eyes froze for a moment.

"She waited patiently and it suited me," he continued. "I was putting my business first and I thought she understood the passion for my job. I didn't notice when things went wrong. One rainy Sunday I was informed that she got engaged to somebody else and it hit me. My life fell apart. It made it worse that she and I were in the same circle of friends and family. Wherever I went, I saw or heard about her and I guess I needed an escape. I saw the hotel for sale and immediately decided to buy it. I was in Cornwall only once as a teenager, but I remembered I liked it a lot and wanted to come back here and live in a house overlooking the sea. I also liked that I would have a partner who could take care of business when I had to go to London for a few days or weeks," he finished, looking a little surprised that he'd said so much about himself.

But his story touched her and it was the first time she looked at him as a man, a person, not just her new business partner. He had a soft voice, but appeared strong and it felt as though one could rely on him. She noticed something else, too; every time he smiled his eyes stayed sad. Suddenly she felt that working with him would be easy and that they would be good business partners.

It crossed her mind that they could be more than that, and the ten-years age gap between them wouldn't matter, or maybe it was just what she needed, an older man who would give her the stability and security she was lacking.

"I have a feeling," he said, "that we will get on well as business partners."

\* \* \*

The next day, Garrett came to work at eight o'clock in the morning. He was curious about the hotel and every-thing related to it. It was his first. In London they had a factory which he left in the hands of his father, brother and brother-in-law.

"From today I start working and learning hotel manage-ment. Don't spare me at work," he said with a laugh.

"I won't," she said, laughing with him. "The most important thing is to watch over everything. Preferably from morning to evening. Staff must know we have an eye on everything. Then everyone does their best and the customers are satisfied and give us a good review."

They agreed that they would work shifts. One week he would come earlier and leave earlier and she would come later and leave later and the next week the other way around. They also agreed to have every other weekend off. She found it to be a very good solution, which hadn't been possible to achieve with the Greenbergs, who usually came in at ten in the morning and left at three in the afternoon and refused to hire an extra manager.

As he was getting used to the hotel, Garrett said he was convinced he'd made the right decision by moving to Cornwall. He was delighted with the neighbourhood and said that it felt like he had been born here. He still had to bring his things from London. For now, he was renting a cottage outside of town. He took a few books to read from a small bookcase in the office, about the history of the town and the Castle. He seemed unpretentious, hardworking and was easy to talk to, and Joann felt quite relaxed with him. She noticed, with surprise, that she was quickly getting used to him and his way of being.

He insisted on rebuilding the tower and opening the dungeons, and planned to start the work in early spring. Joann never saw the need for big changes. She knew the castle well, she had been working here for years. She could walk through the corridors with her eyes closed, mastered its management to perfection and felt comfortable in her role, however the thought of change excited her. Garrett taught her something new that it's good to plan ahead and take on new challenges.

She instinctively headed towards the entrance to the dungeons. She remembered how Richard and her with some neighbourhood kids had explored the dungeons years ago when she was about ten. One of the boys got lost there, and was found terrified after a few hours of searching. It was then decided that the dungeons would be shut and the entrance was nailed. She remembered the eerie feeling she had down there in the darkness of the corridors.

The entrance was in a remote part of the castle, a winding steep staircase led down to it. At the top they were fenced off with an iron chain with a sign "Do not enter".

Above the stairs on the wall hung a portrait in a carved frame. It was a portrait of a man of about thirty in aristocratic clothes and a heavy gold chain around his neck assuring his wealth. He had soft, pleasant features and dark curls that fell on his shoulders. His eyes were staring ahead as if wandering in deep thought.

Joann stopped and looked at him for a moment. His character has always intrigued her. She found there was some mystery in his eyes, as if they were hiding a great secret. She unhooked the chain and took a few steps down almost losing balance on the winding stairs. There was no handrail and she thought installing one would be the first thing to do for the safety of the guests. She went down a few stairs, found a switch and turned it on but the light didn't come on.

"The bulb burned out," she said and was about to go back when something moved downstairs. "Who's there?" she asked loudly and continued down, only to find herself in total darkness. "Who's there?" she asked again annoyed by the lack of answer. Now she heard the distinct sound of footsteps and then dead silence. She waited for a moment listening. It got eerily quiet, she felt a strange chill. The same ghastly feeling came over her, and her instinct told her to back off. She hurried upstairs, rushed to the reception and grabbed a flashlight. She absolutely needed to know who was down there.

"Come with me", she said to Alfred, having come across him at the reception.

"This bulb is loose", said Alfred as he tightened the bulb. Bright light illuminated the stone, cold walls with a small, nailed door. There was no trace of anyone's presence here.

"I am sure someone was here", said Joann as they went upstairs.

"It's him", Alfred pointed to the portrait hanging above the stairs.

"Sir Roger?"

"Yes, they say he buried his wife's body down there, so that no one could find her and now he guards this place. This is why his portrait always hangs here, as a warning for others not to come here. A few men died there in these dungeons. I always keep away from this place and advise others to do the same", he said with fear.

# 4

**T**he receptionist called her in the morning to inform her of a theft in the hotel. Joann tried to get there as soon as she could, to find out what exactly happened. Garrett was busy this morning and was going to come to work a little later. Joann decided to take care of it until he arrived, although she didn't particularly like dealing with these kinds of problems. It was one of those things she would normally leave in the hands of Cecilia Greenberg, who would take good care of it.

Alfred was always busy with guests at this time of the day and so she walked to the Castle. It usually took her about twenty minutes to get there. She never learnt to drive. The memories of her father's accident were still too traumatic for her to get behind the wheel.

The morning was sunny. A breeze was blowing and the leaves of the trees were moving slightly in the alley. She passed serene, picturesque cottages with thick walls and painted shutters, and a stony medieval church with a characterful tower. The town had already awoken and there were a lot of people wandering slowly through the sunny, narrow streets. Joann assumed most of them were visitors.

It was breakfast time at the Castle. The restaurant was almost full of guests and the waiters were bustling. The air smelled of hot black coffee and warm freshly-baked croissants dripping with butter. Plates and cutlery rang, people chatted and the atmosphere was relaxed. It was a good sign that customers were satisfied.

"Somebody broke into a display cabinet in the hall upstairs," Connie, the young receptionist, informed her as soon as she walked in. "They smashed the glass and stole two silver candlesticks."

"Damn it," Joann swore loudly on their way upstairs to see the cabinet. It was made from rosewood, engraved with flowers and leaves. The glass had been broken enough to get out the candlesticks. Less valuable porcelain was not taken.

"Do you want me to call the police?" Connie asked.

"I don't need the police here," Jo replied, walking with her hands in the pockets of her trousers. She did this whenever she was annoyed. At the moment, what irritated her most was that one of the employees might have done this and that such thefts could be repeated. They finished examining the cabinet and went back downstairs.

"Maybe they could check to see if there were any fingerprints left," Connie said, trying to convince her. She was a cheerful young woman with reddish-blonde hair and pink cheeks, and she got on well with Joann.

"I suppose you're right. Did anybody see anything?" she asked as they walked down the narrow corridor towards the office.

"No, Jo. Nobody." Connie followed her quick steps.

"What about the chambermaid Millie? She cleans that

part of the hotel. She has been with us for a few months now and there was never any problem with her, was there?" They stood at the office door and Joann put the key in the lock, opened the door and stood with her hand on the doorknob.

"So far no, but her family has been in trouble lately. Her father broke his leg, he can't work and gets only a small benefit, and her brother just lost his job. So, Millie feeds the whole family from her wages. Her parents, brother, his wife and their baby," she replied.

"Call her to the office now," she said and walked inside.

Millie was seventeen, slim and quite small. She came in and looked around the room with confused eyes. Her uniform was white with a fine blue checked pattern, and she seemed shy, but it gave the impression of a nice girl and everybody liked her. Joann asked her to sit down and took the seat across the desk from her.

"Yesterday, Millie," she started, "when you were cleaning upstairs, was the cabinet okay?"

"Yes, it was," she replied. She sat with her hands in her lap and looked at Joann carefully.

"So, someone had to have broken into it in the evening." She supposed that was what had happened.

"Or at night, miss," she said, and for a moment hung her gaze on the large portrait above Joann's head.

"Did you notice anything suspicious? Anything that caught your attention."

"No, nothing."

"Did you see Louise hanging around there, yesterday?" she asked, and for a moment it seemed to Joann that it must have been her.

"Who?"

"A woman, slim, blonde curly hair, pretty?"

"No, I didn't," she replied confidently. "But I saw Mr Edgar."

"Edgar!" Joann leaned forward to make sure she heard it right, then straightened her back. "I cannot imagine him smashing the glass and putting candlesticks under his jacket. What was he doing there?"

"He was visiting a lady in room five," Millie replied.

"Visiting?" Joann repeated, a little confused.

"I mean staying overnight," said Millie. "I mentioned that to Jack and he said that they met at the bar yesterday, had a couple of drinks and then left together."

"Thank you. That's all, Millie." She had heard enough. Although she didn't feel anything for Edgar, she felt slightly devastated. One day he proposed a relationship with her and the next he slept with another woman under her own roof.

"Miss," Millie said, standing up. "I didn't do it. I would never steal anything. I would have cut my hand first."

"Millie," Joann said, putting hand on her shoulder, "I know you didn't do it. I am very happy with the job you do for us. I just had to ask you these questions. And tell your brother to come by. I have some temporary jobs for him if he wants."

When Garrett arrived, they decided to report the incident to the police. They wanted the staff to know they were taking this matter very seriously. Only children's fingerprints were found on the sides of the cabinet, though, left there when running around and touching everything, so they decided not to bother the customers. The mystery of the thieves had not been solved.

\* \* \*

The hotel was hosting a three-day coastal degradation conference. More than a dozen people came from different parts of the country, along with some local participants. They were having a lunch break and Joann went down to check if everything was going alright and to talk to the chef about the menu for tomorrow's feast. The lunch was nearly over. Small groups of people were sitting in the bar and in the parlour having coffee and cold drinks. Two women smiled at her when she walked through the foyer.

"The Castle is absolutely magnificent," a handsome woman with a dark complexion said to her.

"I hope that everything is to your satisfaction," she replied, and sat down with them in the golden parlour.

It was a light room with a marble fireplace and two orna-mental columns on the side. A large mirror hung over the fireplace in a carved golden frame. On the mantel were crystal candlesticks reflecting in the mirror. A Baroque Boutique sofa was covered in aqua green, floral, damask fabric, and it had remarkable carvings finished in gold leaf. It stood by a large, arched stained glass window. In the centre were three small French coffee tables with marble tops and baroque armchairs. A corner, gold leaf French display cabinet held silverware and porcelain. On the wall opposite the fireplace hung a large portrait of a young lady in a light pink ruffled dress with a neckline revealing her shoulders, pink ribbons woven into her golden curls and a bouquet of ash roses in hand. Her face was so alluring that it was impossible not to notice the portrait.

"We haven't seen any ghosts here yet," said the same woman, who introduced herself as Regina. She had deep black eyes and curly black hair nicely pinned up. She was sitting with her husband who was one of the organisers of the conference, he was attractive but looked rather serious. He was sitting close to his wife and together they looked like a handsome couple.

"There are a few ghosts in the Castle," Joann replied, ready to tell a few ghost stories that usually made visitors laugh.

"Have you seen them?" asked a young Scot Lennox sitting at a table next to her.

"I haven't seen them myself," she replied, "but some of our employees and guests have. Most often you can see a woman. We aren't sure who she was, but we think she lived here in the fifteenth century and was Lord Dryden's hated wife. She roams the castle mainly at night, trying to lure lonely men to the top of the tower to push them down. One evening, our night porter saw one of our guests in pyjamas walking towards the tower. When he approached him, the man said that he'd followed a tall woman with long, black, loose hair."

"That's exactly the woman I saw in my dream last night," said Lennox and everybody laughed.

"I wouldn't sleep tonight if I were you," said Regina's husband and everybody laughed again.

"I wouldn't mind if this beauty visited me," said Lennox, pointing to the woman in the portrait. "In fact, I saw someone very similar to her at the Castle bar last evening. Her name was Louise."

Joann fell silent. Whenever she forgot about Louise something always reminded her and the problem resumed again. She wasn't happy that Louise kept coming to the Castle and thought she would have to deal with it somehow.

The lunch break was over and they all walked back to the conference room. Joann was on her way to the office when Edgar caught up with her.

"I need to talk to you, Jo." There was a plea in his voice, quite a change from the last time they spoke.

"What would the woman in room five say to that?" She couldn't help but mention this woman, awaiting his comment.

"She is married, Jo," he replied without any particular remorse over the night spent with a strange woman, and instinctively looked at two young women passing along the hallway. Joann looked at him disappointed thinking she was naive to expect him to show some guilt. She was surprise to notice that she resented him for it and felt hurt.

"I'm going to the office, we can talk there," she said, taking a few steps down the corridor.

"You know I haven't been down to your office since I saw that apparition standing there with the long, black hair and dead eyes. Let's sit at the bar," he pleaded.

There were a few people sitting at the small wooden tables. Jack stood behind the bar, polishing glasses carefully. The room was pleasantly cosy. It had a stone floor and exposed beams on the ceiling. There was a gigantic open fireplace opposite the bar that took up the entire wall, built of red bricks and a heavy oak beam mantel. The eye was drawn to three knightly shields hanging above the fireplace.

The whole room was softly lit by wall lamps and small

ornamental lanterns hanging from the ceiling, building a climate for relaxation. Edgar took a pint of beer and sat down on a monk bench by the wall and Joann on the wooden armchair next to him with a glass of cider.

Garrett entered the bar and waved when he noticed her. He was with George McGrattan who was the Head of Culture and Environment, and another man she didn't know. He'd said that he wanted to meet the locals, make contacts and acquaintances, and he was doing just that.

"That's Garrett Fereday, your new business partner. He's staying at The Corner House at the end of the town," said Edgar and she looked at him, surprised he knew such details. "Funny thing," he continued. "I saw a woman who looked like you standing near his house yesterday when I was driving by at night," he said and took a long sip of beer.

"It wasn't me."

"That's funny, because she looked just like you," he said watching casually as people entered the bar. It was a group of four holidaymakers, two men and two women. The men ordered drinks at the bar while the women found a table.

"Why would I go near his house?" she said, angry by his insinuations and wondering what he hoped to achieve. "If I want to speak to him I can do it here, in the Castle. He will be coming here every day now."

"Maybe it's me. Maybe I just see you everywhere." He looked at her meaningfully, but his words did not move her. On the contrary, they irritated her. They were all lies according to her. She stared out the window for a moment, silently, and looked discreetly at Garrett. He was busy talking.

"You know what is funny," she started, still irritated.

"That the bar is the only place in the Castle where you can be, not being afraid of some apparitions, yet you spent the whole night upstairs in room five, with that woman."

"I don't know myself how it happened, I must have been totally drunk," he replied and took another long sip. It was the most stupid explanation she expected to hear from him. "If we had been together it would never have happened."

But somehow, she was almost sure that it would have happened. That he would have cheated and lied to her all the time and driven her mad.

"That evening I came here hoping to speak to you. I had a few drinks and I don't remember what happened next." He stopped and added after a while, "I can really see you happy with me, Jo."

"Maybe you should just stop drinking, you start to see ghosts," she said sharply. "I have to go. I have lots of paper-work to do. I won't finish till late today."

* * *

Joann had spent the entire afternoon tidying up old papers. She didn't want Garrett to see all this accumulated mess. She wanted him to have a good impression of her. Work with him was going well. He even joked once that they complemented each other, like a good old marriage. She noticed that he often looked at her thoughtfully, but never let her understand that he was emotionally involved in her. She could just make a move first and show him more affection but if he rejected her, the relations between them would worsen and working with him would be unbearable.

However Joann hoped that as they got to know each other better, something more would develop between them.

Although he advised her like a good friend not to work until late, it was evening before she decided to go home. She saw from the window that someone was in a room that was not occupied at the moment and decided to check it out. It was the same room that had flooded a few days earlier and she wondered if Ben was still working at this time. As she opened the heavy door, she was relieved to be right.

"Oh, it's you, Ben," she said. "I saw an open window. Are you still working?" She went inside to see how much work was already done. The fresh smell of paint spread across the room. The ceiling was white and clean and there was new wallpaper on the walls.

"Just finished for today. I stayed a little longer because tomorrow I want to come later, if I may," he said. "I have a little job to do in the morning." The renovation was almost finished and she didn't mind him coming later as long as everything was done on time.

"That's alright, but what is the little job you have to do?" she asked.

"Just repairing an old boat," he explained. "A sailing boat," he pointed out, proudly implying that he also knows how to repair sailing boats. "I promised someone I'd finish it for tomorrow," he added. "There," he pointed his finger at the heavy velvety curtains "have you seen him?" he asked, lowering his voice.

"No, what was it?"

"Him. A ghost. It's the second time he's come and watched me working. Funny looking fellow." He stared at the curtains as if something really was there, but Joann saw no ghost.

"It must be Sir Roger," she assumed, because it was the only male ghost in the castle they knew about.

"Who is he?"

"He lived here with his beautiful wife who he loved dearly," she started. "He had plantations in India and his administrator there was calling him to come. But his wife was expecting a baby and begged him not to leave her till the baby was born. He left but he promised to come back before the baby was due. Unfortunately she lost the baby and sickened. He hurried home but she died just hours before his arrival. He spent two days next to her body and begged her to wake up, promising never to leave her again. They had to drag him away from her and then her body disappeared. Apparently, she was buried with all her expensive jewellery, but no one knew where her grave was. Then he started to drink heavily and was killed in a duel which he attempted while drunk," she finished. She went to the window and corrected the curtain.

"What a dreadful story," he commented and shuddered. He looked around the room, slightly scared, but the ghost didn't appear anymore.

"I have never seen him but some people have. Are you scared of ghosts?"

"Not that much, you see my mother's sister was married to a gravedigger and I helped him as a boy, and now and then he gave me a shilling," he answered. "I've seen a lot but they cannot do much to you, once they are dead. They just stare at you. Like this." He made staring eyes.

"Was it here in Cornwall?" she asked.

"No, on the Irish coast," he said proudly and smiled at the thought of the beautiful, old land.

"Irish coasts are beauteous and the people are nice," she stated appreciatively.

"Have you been?"

"Yes, but a long time ago. We spent our vacation there with my parents." She made a move towards the door. "I'd better go home, my poor mother is bored on her own."

"Miss," he said hesitantly, "if there is any other job at the estate, mowing grass or cutting hedges, you will let me know, won't you?"

"Of course, Ben, I will."

"Would you like me to walk you to the estate, miss?" he asked. "It is getting late."

"No, thank you." How very kind of him, she thought.

# 5

oann walked through the chestnut alley leading to her house. The large, old trees with thick trunks grew on both sides, their crowns touching here and there to form a vault overhead. The leaves had begun to turn yellow and brown and thorny fruits were large and ripe. The sun was low but it was still bright, breaking through the branches that shadowed the alley and its rays were playing on the ground. But one could already feel the dampness in the air. Joann felt a sudden gust of cold wind heralding autumn.

She heard a strange noise behind her and turned abruptly, but the alley was empty and the noise stopped. She stood listening but the sound never came back. She wondered if it could have been a bird or a squirrel, but somehow she got the feeling of being followed, watched, and a shiver passed down her spine. She walked faster towards the house, looking around, but there was no one.

The dogs heard her and ran up to welcome her, wagging their tails in joy, and she patted them to let them know that she missed them too. A hunched figure appeared in the hall, happy to see her back home.

"Are you hungry?" she asked. Like every mother, she

thought that everybody must be fed.

"No, but I'll make a cup of tea. Would you like one too?" Joann asked her.

"Yes, but let me do it," she said and went to the kitchen.

Joann had had a long day and it was nice to come back home to rest. She went to the large lounge and poured herself a glass of Chardonnay. Her mother entered the lounge carrying a silver tray with a teapot and two cups. The aroma of hot, strong tea filled the room and made her forget about the unpleasant moment in the alley. She took the tray, put it on the small coffee table and poured two cups. She gave one to her mother, who was already sitting in the comfortable armchair in front of the patio door, and Joann took the other armchair.

"How was your day, Mum?" She stretched her legs out, put her feet on the footrest and rested her head on the high back of the chair.

"The Greenbergs came to say goodbye. They are leaving tomorrow," she said, worried. "How sad. We'll probably never see them again." She took out a handkerchief and wiped her nose.

"Cecilia said they would call and write and send photos. We could visit them next summer if you like," Joann said, trying to cheer her up when she saw her dejected face. She was afraid she would get another bout of apathy.

"Nonsense," her mother said. "Edgar's mother called," she changed the subject. "She invited us for dinner and talked a lot about Edgar. I will tell you in secret that she hopes that something will bring you closer together and I think so too"

"It is too late for that. "Joann thought for a moment. She already believed once that they were meant to be together, but his constant interest in women frustrated her and her hopes slowly faded away, leaving her indifferent towards him. There was no chance of returning her former feelings. "He has changed a lot and I don't recognize him sometimes," she said after a while.

"Give him a chance. It is such a good match for you. Promise me you will think about it."

"All right. I will," she answered to finish the subject.

"How was the hotel today?"

"Busy, and everything was fine. Our handyman saw Sir Roger's ghost today," said Jo, trying to arouse her interest. She knew her mother liked all kinds of ghost stories and she often told them to the hotel guests with pleasure, to entertain them.

"Sir Roger? No. That's not possible."

"Why not?"

"Because Sir Roger's ghost is looking for his beloved wife and he appears only to women. No man has ever seen him." She finished her tea and set the empty cup on the table.

"But Ben just saw him twice," Joann said, convinced it had to be him.

"It wasn't him. It must have been somebody else," her mother insisted.

"Who do you think it was?"

"Oh, I don't know, I don't know. I'll go and lie down. I am very tired."

\* \* \*

That night, Joann had a nightmare. A dark grey spirit was hunting her. She was running down the stairs, terrified, and the ghost was right behind her, howling frighteningly. She jumped up from her sleep, scared, and sat on the bed in the dark. The dogs were barking fiercely downstairs and she leapt to her feet, terrified that something had happened.

Without thinking, she ran down the stairs in the dark, to the lounge, where the noise was coming from. The patio doors were wide open and her mother was standing there in a nightgown, looking out into the night. The dogs were with her, barking furiously at the darkness. Joann called them to come and they ran up to her obediently, then went out again, as if something was bothering them in the garden. Something or someone, lurking in hiding, watching.

It seemed that something would emerge from the trees in a moment. She looked around, horrified. Dark, stormy clouds obstructed the moon and one could not see anything out there, only dark shapes of trees blowing in the gusty, cold wind. The wooden gate must have broken because it started hitting the fence and the dull thumping sound spread throughout the garden. Joann embraced her mother. The woman was frozen. The wind was wailing and grew stronger, tugging at her hair, and the darkness outside was impenetrable, making her shiver again. A sudden flash of lightning lit the dark sky and then a loud thunderclap. They both flinched. She brought her mother inside, called the dogs in and closed the door, locking it with a key. A huge downpour came and, after a while, another lightning strike and thunder. She took the frozen woman to the kitchen, covered her with a blanket and put the kettle on. They sat at the table. A small lamp gave enough light. It was 2AM.

"I saw him, Jo. He was here," she said, half happy, half scared.

"Who, Mum?" she asked, worried and still shivering with cold.

"Henry. Your father. His spirit was here. I knew it was him when you told me about Ben seeing the ghost." She was very anxious and her face seemed to be hot.

"Dad is in heaven," Joann said gently, trying to calm her down.

"No, he cannot be. I saw him, he wore his same favourite dark jacket. He paced the patio and then faded into the darkness. He always liked to walk alone in the garden, especially at dusk, delving into his thoughts," she insisted, excited.

"Why would he come now?" asked Joann, trying to find out what was going on in her mother's mind. For many years she had suffered from nervous breakdowns and depression that recurred with increasing frequency. Joann had brought doctors to treat her and did her best to support her, but she felt more and more powerless.

"His spirit is here because I killed him," her mother said, openly and firmly.

"Mum, please. Dad died in a car accident eleven years ago," she said it in a pleading voice as if the woman in front of her was crazy and she wanted to bring her mind to the present. She put both hands on her mother's small palms and held them gently.

"Your father had an affair with a servant," she revealed and paused for a moment, as if the memory had caused her sudden pain. "He had a dark side which nobody knew. He was secretly doing strange business and sometimes went away for days. When he came back, I saw him counting large amounts of money which he later turned into precious stones." She instinctively touched her emerald necklace. "He was obsessed with it, he only believed in precious stones and gold. I didn't know anything about the business he was doing and I didn't interfere with those matters, but when he got involved with this girl and lost his head for her I couldn't forgive him. I was afraid of a scandal. I prayed on my knees for justice and God heard me and he died. Because I wanted it." She covered her face with her hands and sobbed quietly. Suddenly she raised her face and said, "I knew that one day he would be back seeking my forgiveness, because he cannot rest without it."

Joann fell silent. She remembered her childhood and the figure of her father. Her memories of him were always warm. He was energetic and busy, but smiling and caring towards them. He often spent time with them when Richard and her were playing in the garden. Joann would put her dolls on the blanket next to the juniper trees and her father would sit on the large stone and tell her nursery rhymes he knew by heart. She still remembered his favourite rhyme,

*'Mary, Mary quite contrary*
*How does your garden grow?*
*With silver bells and cockleshells*
*And pretty maids all in a row'.*

He left a void in their home and in her heart that she realised she still felt. She was not prepared for what she'd just heard about him and her mind struggled to accept it. She looked at her mother. There was a painful expression on her face and Joann squeezed her hand gently. They were silent for a while.

"What happened to the precious stones and gold after his death?" she asked.

"I don't know," her mother answered. Her eyelids began to droop slowly and Joann noticed that she was very tired.

"Were they not in the safe?"

"No. The safe was empty." She put her head on her hand and closed her eyes.

"You need to go to bed, Mum. Let me take you." She took her by the arm and walked her to her bedroom. When she returned to her own room, she looked at the clock. She could still get a few hours of sleep and decided to go to bed, hoping to drift off straight away. Thoughts raced through her head. She saw the image of her father before her eyes. He had her in his arms when she was a chubby little girl. Then she saw him sitting at the desk with the table lamp lit, counting money. At last she fell asleep wearily.

The next day, Joann woke up late. She put her clothes on and went downstairs. Her mother was pottering about the kitchen and chatting with the cook who came for a few hours to prepare some meals. Her name was Mildred and she was a serious middle-aged woman.

"Have some breakfast," her mother said. "I don't like when you get up late and leave the house hungry."

"Yes, I will," she replied and sat down at the table. Her mother took a plate of hot omelette and two pieces of toast that had just been prepared by Mildred and put it on the table in front of her. Mildred brought the teapot and made her a cup of tea.

"Thank you, that's sweet of you," she said.

Joann noted with joy that her mother was in a good mood and there was no trace of last night's events on her face. She chose not to mention it.

"Why don't you come to the Castle for lunch today?" she asked, looking at her watch and knowing that she'd be late for work. She put a large piece of toast in her mouth.

"I have lunch in town today, with Dorothy," she answered cheerfully.

"That's a great idea. You will certainly have a nice time. Give her my regards," said Joann. She finished eating in a hurry and ran out of the house.

Her mother's words about the gold and stones hidden somewhere there echoed in her mind. She realized well how much it would help her and change her life. If she only knew where to look for them. She had a feeling these restless thoughts would stay with her for a long time.

# 6

t **was the** last day of the coastal degradation conference and they were having a small feast in the evening at the hotel. They ordered a continental buffet; cold meats, a selection of cheeses, olives, tomatoes and prawn salads, stroganoff, risotto and eel soup. Joann went down to the Gothic room to check if the preparations were going smoothly. She wanted everything to be done on time and to look great. George McGrattan was invited, together with his wife and a few other personalities, and she had to impress them with an excellent quality of service.

Everything was nearly ready. The long table was covered with a white tablecloth. A large crystal bowl filled with fruit stood in the centre of the table between two low vases of flowers, orange carnations, red gerberas, blue asters and chrysanthemums. The food was put on silver plates and in porcelain bowls. The tutti frutti meringue cake stood on a crystal stand, eclairs and cupcakes on crystal plates and drinks on silver trays. Candlesticks had been lit and smooth, classical music played in the background. The guests were about to arrive. Joann and Garrett were invited, which was a nice gesture from the organiser, Paul Dalton, whom she had known for years.

Joann wondered for a long time what to wear. She wanted Garrett to see her in a different light than every other day, to charm him with her appearance. She put on a bias cut, floor-length silk gown in midnight blue with slit sleeves and a sapphire necklace and earrings. She waved her hair and put light pink blusher on her cheeks that matched nicely with her pale complexion. The powdery scent of her perfume wafted softly. Looking at the mirror in the hall, she felt beautiful and she hoped that Garrett would notice.

The guests started to come down and Paul welcomed them, introducing her to some of his friends. Garrett turned up late. He looked just like she had imagined him on the first day, in a black, perfectly cut tuxedo.

"You look beautiful," he said to her. She looked into his eyes and found sincere delight, then she smiled at him flirtatiously.

A few people approached them and Garrett was drawn into a business conversation with George McGrattan and the conference organisers. She didn't speak to him much that evening. She looked at him from a distance as he engaged with various people. Sometimes she noticed him watching her and their eyes met for a moment. She noticed that a woman was also watching her. Joann didn't know her but thought that she must have been one of the conference participants.

The guests mainly talked to her about the Castle. They praised the food and marvelled at the town and marina. Regina complained that her husband often travelled on business trips to seaports all over the country. He worked in the

Maritime Ministry and was preparing a program of protection for sea shores.

Lennox, as it turned out, was about thirty years old. He worked in Scotland in the Maritime Office and was the Deputy Director. He was much taller than her and well built. He came dressed in a long sleeved traditional araca jacket, waistcoat, tie and a blue-and-green tartan kilt. He told her about Scotland, recalling how he fished with his grandfather among the magical scenery of dramatic ancient woodland, how they watched local wildlife and stargazed at warm summer nights. He seemed very intelligent with a deep affection for Scotland and very much likeable.

He was leaving early the next day and they promised that they would remain in touch, and he held her firmly in his arms for goodbye. Regina also said she would call her to complain about her husband and numerous of other things, and told Joann that she must come and visit her in London. Joann was happy for the invitation, as she already liked this cheerful woman. It got late and the guests began to diverge. George McGrattan and his wife also said goodbye and went home. Joann was about to leave when the woman who had been watching her for some time came up to her.

"I wanted to thank you for the good service and comfortable room," she said and her voice sounded very haughty.

"Which room did you stay in?" asked Joann. It was always nice to hear that the guests were satisfied.

"In room five," she replied. "With the antique French furniture. It makes an imposing impression indeed."

The lady from room five. Where had she heard this before? Now she remembered. The woman that Edgar had spent a night with, or nights. She was surprised by her appearance. So far Edgar's prey were simple, local girls, madly in love with him. But the woman from room five was elegant, had a fancy taste and wore expensive perfume. She had an oriental beauty with slightly slanted eyes and full mouth covered in ruby lipstick. She looked very interesting and attracted the eyes of men.

"I really wanted to meet you because Edgar told me a lot about you." She took a sip of Martini, measuring Joann from the top to the bottom with a cold gaze. "Actually he talks about you all the time," she added, waiting for Joann's reply.

"He is a friend of the family," she explained.

"Oh, yes. I know just what he is." She took another sip. "He also said that both your parents planned to marry you together."

Joann didn't quite understand what all these strange comments were about.

"That is how our parents joked when we were kids," she said with a nice tone of voice, even though the woman was starting to annoy her.

"I hope so," she said, "because I have crush on him and when I want something I get it."

"I wish you both happiness then," said Joann without moving a single muscle on her face. "If you'll excuse me, my duties are calling me." She was irritated enough but didn't want it to show.

"It was fun meeting you," she replied.

"The pleasure was mine," said Joann and gave her a cold smile.

The woman took a final dismissive look at her, turned around and went to join a pair of guests standing nearby.

Joann left, agitated by this unexpected conversation and the nonchalant behaviour of the woman from room five.

Garrett caught up with her at the hotel front door while she waited for Alfred.

"I'll give you a lift home," he said. She looked at him, surprised by his sudden appearance. She'd waited all evening for an opportunity to talk to him, which somehow hadn't happened, and now he appeared so unexpectedly that she felt a little dazed.

"It's dark," he said with a smile. "And it has started to rain."

"Thank you," she said, smiling back at him. It felt nice that he thought about her and had decided to leave the party to take her home. It was indeed raining and they walked quickly to his car. He opened the door for her then got behind the wheel and they drove away. She looked through the window. The streets were empty. The roadside lanterns glowed illuminating the wet road and droplets of failing rain.

"Did you enjoy the party?" he asked.

"Yes, I did. I think that our chefs and service did a good job again," she said with conviction and satisfaction that everything had gone well. They were silent for a minute and there was only the hum of the engine. "Don't you think so?" she asked.

"Yes, the food was excellent. The guests praised it. What about your Scotch friend?" he asked, clearly having noticed that she'd spent almost the entire evening in his company.

"He was a very nice man," she replied honestly. But even

though he was nice and seemed to like her she knew that this acquaintance had no future. The distance alone would make such a relationship impossible. She would never leave her glorious Castle to move closer to him and he would never leave his beloved Scotland to live with her in Cornwall.

"He had rather a good pair of legs," Garrett said with another smile, and he looked at her, waiting for her reaction, but she didn't find that comment funny.

"He had a good sense of humour, too," she replied and he laughed.

He stopped the car by the front door of the house. In the dark, its magnificent proportions could not be seen. The lights of the car illuminated only its sumptuous entrance. The rain intensified and drummed against the car windshields.

"The lights are off," he said looking at the house.

"That means that Mum is already in bed."

"I won't wake her up then. I will pop in and meet her another day."

"Would you like to visit us this Sunday for dinner?" she asked.

"I would love to." He thought for a moment. "But I have to go to London this weekend. My father and brother-in-law take care of the business there, but there are a few things I want to talk to them about. But maybe the next Sunday," he proposed.

"That would be wonderful," she replied.

"That's settled then," he said and looked into her eyes for a moment.

"Yes. Goodnight." She hesitated, wondering if he would move closer to kiss her, but he didn't. She left the car and went to the front door of the house. She put a hand on the doorknob and turned to look at him. He was still sitting in the car. The rain was pouring down the glass making it impossible to recognise the expression on his face. She went inside, closed the door and leaned her back against it. She heard the sound of the engine quickly moving away.

# 7

**T**he morning started sunny, though a bit cold. Puddles remained after yesterday's rain and there was still a fresh, wet smell in the air. Joann put on a knee-length skirt and a light, short jacket fastened with a wide belt. She looked up at the cloudless sky and hoped that despite the cold wind the day would get warmer. The birds sang beautifully in the alley and she remembered the old saying "The littlest birds sing the sweetest songs. "She smiled, the day seemed nice to her. She was walking joyfully, lightly jumping over the puddles. She thought about Garrett last night and was glad she would see him soon. The hotel was almost empty as the guests were leaving early. Suitcases were in the hall, blocking the aisle. Alfred struggled with them as he took some of the guests to the station. One couple in travelling outfits was making loud calls on the phone at the reception attracting everyone's attention.

The aroma of strong, black coffee came from the restaurant and she thought she must have some. She went to the restaurant and made herself a cup, carrying it back to her office. She walked in happy, expecting to find Garrett there reading the newspaper, but he wasn't. Instead she found a beautiful bouquet of freesias on the table, smelling softly, and she wondered if he had brought them. The phone rang and she answered it. It was Connie, the hotel receptionist.

"Unannounced customers came to see the Gothic room to arrange a wedding. Garrett went with them to show them around. He asked if you could join them when you arrive."

"Okay, thank you, Connie." She went immediately, with quick, decisive steps. She knew that he was new to these booking matters and might need help. She met them at the Gothic room. It was a young couple and the bride's parents. Garrett looked at her with relief and joy. There was something gentle in his look too, but she wasn't sure what exactly it meant.

The Gothic room was tidy, cleaned and dusted, and there was no trace of yesterday's reception. It was a stately hall with four stone columns supporting a dome-shaped vault giving an impression of splendour. It was panelled with a dark wood. On the right side of the entrance was a bar, and on the left a long, heavy wooden table with gothic chairs upholstered in red, and a few square tables. Behind, two steps below, was a square dance floor, then French glazed doors with large windows overlooking the garden where guests, tired of dancing, could go to refresh themselves. The interior captivated with its antique features and decorations, especially the various portraits on the walls. The guests were appreciative of the magnificent stone fireplace with marble carvings and a large-scale painting handing above. It was a painting of a sunny orangery with exotic sprawling plants. Against the glass wall there stood a piano with a young girl paying on it. On soft fluffy sofas sat ladies and gentlemen dressed in medieval clothes and three dogs rested lazily at their feet. The orangery looked like oasis of peace where they could relax among greenery and subtle music and the guests admired the picture with delight.

They looked around, fascinated by the hall and the Castle. Garrett offered them a drink and they all sat at the long table. The waiter brought tea and coffee. It took some time to discuss the details and choose the menu but the customers left satisfied. Joann noticed that Garrett listened attentively when she spoke. He looked at her often and she was beginning to believe that he saw in her something more than just a business partner. They went back to the foyer chatting. It was calmer and empty now.

"Have all conference participants already left?" she asked Connie as they passed by reception desk.

"Everyone except the lady from the five room. She extended her stay for a few days," Connie informed her and Joann subconsciously wondered if this arrogant woman would cause some trouble. "Some new guests have already arrived," Connie continued.

Joann smiled at the news. The season was not over yet. All the rooms were booked and she expected the hotel to be full again this evening.

"The freesias look beautiful," she said when they entered the office.

"These are my favourite flowers," he said. "I thought you might like them."

"I absolutely love them, they are my favourites too," she replied, looking deeply into his eyes. His gaze was very calm, but something disturbed her, there was still no happiness in his eyes. They ordered a hot lunch and ate together at a table outside, talking mostly about business. The sun was high and the sky was still clear. It got warmer and nicer.

In the afternoon, when Joann was sorting out the invoices, she noticed one large order for a new type of wine. She decided to find Garrett and ask him about it, wondering if it was a mistake or something he ordered and forgot to tell her about. He was supposed to check the menu with the chef, but he was not there. She went to the bar. Garrett was sitting with George McGrattan again and she decided not to bother him at the moment.

The woman from room five was alone at the bar with a drink. She stared ahead and drank in small sips. Joann decided to leave before she accosted her, rushing back to the door leading to the Castle hall. She heard the main bar door open and turned to see who it was. She expected it to be Edgar coming to meet that woman, but to her surprise she saw Louise. She'd forgotten about her and now she appeared again unexpectedly like an evil spirit that disturbs the peace of the household and won't go away. Joann thought that if her mother were here now she would be devastated.

She decided she would speak to Louise and tell her not to come to the Castle again, hoping that she would understand and leave them alone. She didn't have the heart to do it now, though, and decided to visit her cottage tomorrow morning.

Louise stood at the bar and ordered two glasses of wine, one red one and one white. She looked around the room. There weren't too many people here yet and she was pleased to see that her favourite table by the fireplace was free. A woman of oriental beauty sitting next to her at the bar watched her out of the corner of her eye.

"Are you going to drink it all yourself?" she asked her casually.

"No. The white wine is for my late friend, Richard. Today is the anniversary of our first meeting and I wanted to celebrate it with him at the table where we used to sit," Louise explained.

"You mean you want to have a drink with a dead man?" the woman asked.

"Yes," Louise replied, a bit embarrassed about her reaction, and took the glasses.

"It's very touching," the woman said coldly. She put a cigarette holder in her mouth and puffed. "Just give me a shout to join you if people look strangely at you. I'm Jessica."

"I'm Louise." She smiled at her and went to sit down at the table. She set the glass of white wine in front of her by the empty chair.

# *8*

*I*n the morning, before work, Joann went to see Louise. She decided to talk to her once and for all and forbid her from coming to the Castle. As she walked, her tension and readiness to settle the matter grew, and she was sure she would achieve her goal. She knew that Louise's house was one of the last on this part of the coast. She walked up the paved road that narrowed and began to turn treacherous. Finally, a little cottage emerged on a rocky hill above a small bay. It was so small she thought that the bedrooms must be in the attic.

When she came closer she saw that the cottage was shrouded in red rose bushes and sweet peas that climbed the walls around the front door. The front garden was extensive and densely covered with purple and red flowers. Roses, vibrant purple lollipops, rich rosy asters, violettas with flowers of the deepest purple, exotic rose-pink cleomes and pink and purple heathers made the whole garden look like a field of purple and red. The sight took her breath away and she had to stop and take a deep breath. She smelled a slightly sweet fragrance surrounding her, a mix of herbs and flowers. She could hear the sea, which now seemed bluer than ever before.

Joann felt a sudden weakness, as though she'd lost her strength for this conversation, doubting its positive result. She tried to arouse her long-standing firmness, but unsuccessfully. She took another deep breath, went to the front door and knocked. After a while, the door opened and she saw Louise. The woman looked surprised to see her but invited her inside. She was wearing a light blue silk dressing gown which, as she walked, revealed her pale shapely legs clad in silver low-heeled shoes.

Joann expected the cottage to be dark and dull but she was surprised again. The sitting room was painted white and the rear wall was completely glazed, glass doors were leading out to the garden, giving the room a bright, airy feel. There was a comfortable-looking couch, armchairs and two coffee tables with lamps on them, and a large standing lamp by the couch. A stone inglenook with a double-door iron stove occupied the side wall. The back garden was smaller and descended gently down to the bay. It was completely possessed by climbing roses and sweet peas, stretching towards the glass doors, and they seemed like they were trying to break inside through the glass.

The sea blended with the blue of the sky, and in the distance boats with white sails swayed gently on the waves. Gulls circled overhead, crying out. Joann thought that during storms the waves must come quite close to the cottage, hitting rocks loudly, and she thought that one must have courage to live in such a place. Louise offered her a drink but she declined and didn't want to sit down.

"I saw you in the Castle yesterday, in the bar," she said,

watching Louise as she poured herself some lemonade.

"Yes, I used to sit there with Richard, in front of the fireplace, and spin yarns. Some places in the Castle are dear to me," she replied, with a hint of nostalgia in her voice.

"My mum goes to the Castle sometimes for morning tea. It could upset her if she saw you there. The news of your return has already distressed her enough and I'm worried about her health which has deteriorated recently," Joann said.

Louise went to the window and looked at the sea thoughtfully for a while, and seemed to have forgotten about Joann's presence. Then she turned to face her. "I can promise you that I won't go there in the morning, but I would like to pop in sometimes in the evening. I sense Richard's strong presence in the Castle, as if he had been there waiting for me all these years."

It seemed absurd to Joann and she didn't want to compromise. She wanted to make sure that her sick mother's feelings would not get hurt. She wanted to protect her. This is what she had come here for. Louise's soft approach gave her a psychological edge and she dared to take advantage of it.

"This is rather ridiculous, don't you think? To become so attached to a childhood love that was not even real," she said.

"You are wrong. Richard and I really loved each other. We were planning to get married and we signed up in secret." Louise looked at her despairingly.

"Richard never loved you. Do you think that if a man loves a woman he lets her go just like that? Without fighting for her?" she asked brusquely, and Louise's face crumpled with sorrow.

"Richard couldn't oppose your mother," she tried to explain. "That is why we hid our affair for so long, hoping that your mother would warm up and change her mind, but it didn't happen. Not even when she came to speak to me."

"My mother spoke to you?" This was the first Joann had heard about it.

"Yes, your mother came to me, just like you have now. I was only twenty at the time, full of complexes, and she made me feel worthless. She said that I didn't deserve him and that I was ruining his life and the great plans for the future she had for him. That felt awful. I wanted to die. I couldn't stay here and not see him, so I decided to leave. It took me a long time to overcome these traumatic memories and return here." She tried to find some understanding in her eyes but Joann remained cold and distant, despite Louise's confession.

"Why did you come back?"

"Why? Well this is a free country. I have a right to live here if I want to." She shrugged.

"But you have no right to bother us in the Castle, and if I see you there again I will have to turn you out," Joann said with anger.

"You better have a damn good reason for that, because I will sue you if you do. I am not twenty anymore. I'm stronger now and I will stand up for myself."

"What do you want? Money?"

"You and your family. It's all about money for you, isn't it?" Louise walked over, slightly swaying her hips, and stood in front of her. "You have no feelings, do you?" she continued. "And if you by any chance wonder why you have never loved anybody it is because you wouldn't know how."

The slap against Louise's cheek was quick and unexpected, aimed by Joann in a fit of sudden anger, and she herself seemed surprised by that loss of self-control. There was moment of stupor afterward, and for a fraction of a second, both stood motionless in silence.

"Leave my house now," said Louise coldly and loudly.

Joann said nothing. She turned around and left with a quick step.

Louise went to the back garden and sat down on the bench with her legs tucked up. She pushed aside the curls that fell over her eyes, rested her head on her hand and looked at the sea that her and Richard had always liked so much. She did not feel anger, but she was sorry that the conversation with Joann had turned out this way, she thought sadly that Richard wouldn't want to see them arguing.

* * *

On her way back, Joann walked quickly, still agitated, analysing the visit in her mind. She calmed down as she approached the hotel. Garrett was in the office sorting orders. Joann relaxed at the sight of him, forgetting about the conversation she'd had with Louise.

"Samples of French wine came," he said. "And tomorrow morning another couple comes to see the Castle, planning a wedding in spring. I'll take care of them." He looked up at her and went back to the papers.

"I thought you were going to London for the weekend tomorrow, to talk to your father and brother-in-law about the factory," she said, a little confused by his sudden change of plan. She went to her desk and sat down.

"I decided to stay. You can take the weekend off if you want. Your mother will be pleased. I will take care of everything here." He put down some papers and signed the invoice.

"If you're not going to London then why not come to us for dinner this Sunday?"

"Oh, that would be really nice, but unfortunately I will not be able to visit you this weekend. Let's leave it for the next one as we planned earlier," he said quickly without emotions, and it made her feel sad and disappointed. For a moment she wondered why he could not visit them if he wasn't going to London.

The phone rang and Connie let them know that two men wanted to talk to them privately, and Garrett told her to lead them to a private room. It was two well-built men in elegant dark suits and they had Liverpool accents. They both had very serious expressions as if something bad had happened.

"This case is very discreet," one of them began.

"You can count on our discretion," said Garrett.

"My brother's wife, Jessica Brixton, was here for a conference and stayed in this hotel, in room five. She was supposed to come back yesterday, but she extended her stay. We are made to understand that she met a man here and is having an affair with him. Her husband, my brother, wants to know who the man is. I would be obliged if you would help us in this matter."

Garrett looked at Joann but she was silent. "I fully understand the seriousness of the matter, but unfortunately I am not able to help," he said. "We do not get involved in private matters of our clients and I don't know who Mrs Brixton was meeting here. Do you know?" he asked Joann.

"No, I don't," she replied.

The men clearly didn't believe them, and now fierceness appeared on their faces.

"I hoped you could be just a little more helpful," he said.

"We know nothing about it," said Garrett. "Maybe there is some other explanation. It is best to talk to her."

"You won't mind if we ask the staff?" he insisted.

"Of course I cannot forbid you from talking politely to my staff, but you must understand that then the rumours will spread all over the town immediately."

They realised there was nothing else to say and stood up. Garrett escorted them to the door and Joann went back to the office. She phoned Edgar to let him know about the unpleasant situation. She had known him since childhood and since Richard had passed away she'd treated him sometimes like an older brother. Despite the recent misunderstandings, she felt she had to let him know so that he would be prepared to talk to those men. The phone was busy every time she tried, so she resolved to go find him herself.

* * *

The indoor bowling club wasn't busy, two pairs were training for a local competition. Edgar's parents were sitting at a table with a young woman and a child, all of them drinking tea, but he wasn't there. She approached them and said hello.

"What a lovely surprise," Edgar's father, Harold, said.

"It's good to see you," said Edgar's mother, Ethel. "You should visit us more often. Why don't you sit down with us?"

Joann sat at their table. Ethel pushed a plate of biscuits towards her, and she took one.

"Did you come to train for the competition next week?" asked Harold.

"No. I came to talk to Edgar," she replied and looked around at the old familiar room. She remembered she used to play here every day as a teenager when she still secretly had a crush on Edgar and it had seemed to her that they would be a perfect couple but he never really noticed her for years. Now it seemed like a long time ago.

"Edgar is checking supplies in the backroom and will be out soon," said Ethel. "He will be thrilled to see you. I have invited your mother for dinner on Sunday, I hope you will come too," she said seriously. Joann confirmed with a smile and a nod and the lines on Ethel's face relaxed. These were the facial features of a clever woman. Ethel had a head for business and successfully invested her and her husband's money. However, she neglected the upbringing of her only son Edgar. He was left under the watchful eye of ever-changing governesses when both parents were preoccupied with business.

"I am waiting for Edgar too. He promised Archie he'd take him on the merry-go-round," said the woman sitting next to them with a little three-year-old boy on her lap. Only now she recognises her as Lucy, the milkman's daughter. The boy was the son of her sister who had died in childbirth. The boy's father had married again and had no interest in Archie, so he was brought up by Lucy's parents. They were from low class. Her mother stayed at home taking care of seven children. The father kept the family with a hard hand, which, however with time softened and after the death of his daughter he devoted his life to supporting others. Lucy gave an impression of a phlegmatic and composed woman, but she knew what she wanted from life and how to take care of herself.

"I don't understand my son," Ethel said, turning to Lucy. "Why does he make such promises to you? People might think that you are going to get engaged if they see you together all the time."

"I expect him to propose shortly," Lucy replied.

"You are expecting too much, my dear." Ethel shrugged off. "He will never propose to you. He would never do this to me. Over my dead body."

"Whatever it takes," Lucy replied firmly but calmly.

"Harold, did you hear what the girl just said? I guess I'll pass out in a moment," she said to her husband, and then to Lucy, "You are not trying to say that you are expecting…"

"No, I am not expecting his child," she replied. "Not yet anyway."

"I do not mind," said Harold. "If she makes him stop drinking and take care of family business."

"I will take care of the business together with Edgar," said Lucy with voice full of faith and conviction. "It will bring you twice as much money as it does now and more London customers will come here."

"I doubt it," said Ethel. "If people found out that you run the business, we would lose our best clientele."

Joann watched this young, feisty woman with a glimmer of respect for how she was getting her way so fiercely. Although she was not sure what she would achieve by this.

"I'll go and find him," Joann said and stood up.

Edgar was in the back smoking a cigarette and closing a cupboard filled with fresh goods.

"What the hell brings you here?" he asked, looking surprised but pleased to see her. "You haven't been here for ages."

"I came to talk to you." She walked over to him. "And warn you that two men were asking for you concerning this woman, Jessica Brixton. Her husband wants to know who she had the affair with," she said baldly. She wanted him to realise that affairs with married women can have serious consequences. He turned towards her with a strange stony expression on his face.

"What did you tell them?" he asked nervously.

"Nothing, but it won't take them long to find out if they really want to," she answered. She put her hands in her pockets and took a few steps back and forth. "What are you going to do? What are your intentions with her?" She wanted to find out how involved he was with this woman, whether they were making any plans together. She was worried about him. He may be spoiled, but he wasn't bad. She even thought she had been a bit too hard on him lately.

"I have no intentions whatsoever with her," he said, and shook his head. "I told you, I was completely drunk. I have not seen her since."

"She waited for you at the bar yesterday."

"Yesterday I was with Lucy," he confessed hesitantly. He put out his cigarette in the ashtray. "I'll go on vacation and wait until things die down, but I don't want to go alone."

"Why don't you take Lucy with you?"

"Lucy? If I took her with me I would come back with a wedding ring on my finger." He rubbed his face with his hand.

"Well then, maybe you will finally learn not to give women any false hope."

"I did not promise Lucy anything," he denied quickly.

"But you promised Archie you'd take him on the merry-go-round and it's bad enough that his own father fails him."

They left the backroom and slowly walked over to the others. Edgar mussed up the little boy's hair and gave him a piggyback ride. A big smile appeared on Lucy's face and Joann noticed from the way they looked at each other that there was something more between them. She thought if Lucy had not been poor, or Edgar rich, there would be no obstacles for them to get married.

# 9

It was **Saturday** and Joann took the weekend off, as agreed with Garrett. She woke up early and, after breakfast, went to town to look at the shops. Despite the early hour, the town was already quite crowded. It was partly due to the fine weather. Forecasters announced that it would be another beautiful weekend at the end of summer, cloudless and sunny. Narrow paved streets and stone fences shaded by tall shrubs were not warmed by the sun yet and gave off a slight chill, but there was no wind and in the full sun it was pleasantly warm.

The cafes and tea shops were already opened and small tables with colourful umbrellas were lined up in a row on the pavement by the main entrance. People sat lazily on chairs sipping drinks and eating snacks, watching the passing crowd with little interest. Visiting holidaymakers filled the tiny souvenir shops, staring at the shelves and choosing postcards.

Joann stopped at a large shop window displaying evening dresses. A long dress decorated with silver llamas on a slim-shaped mannequin attracted her attention. It tightened the silhouette and had a fancy cut showing the leg up to the knee. She found it captivating, went inside and made her way up the stairs to ask the dark-haired, bored-looking sales-person if she could try the dress on. When she looked in the mirror, she found that it fit perfectly and only needed a minor touch-up. The price was staggering, but it didn't bother her. The longer she looked, however, the more the dress seemed too shiny and defiant, not quite her style.

"But this dress is absolutely stunning!" said a famil-iar-sounding voice, loud and lofty. Joann turned and saw Jessica Brixton behind her.

"I'm not sure, I can't decide really," Joann said, without emotion.

"But you have to have it, of course. Everybody does. That's the fashion now. Silver or golden gowns are a must." She gently touched the material. "This fits your face perfectly and if you don't buy it, you will surely regret it."

Joann agreed and finally decided to buy it. They went upstairs to the shop's cafe and ordered coffee and chocolate ice cream with lots of cream. They were sitting at a table by the window overlooking the sea. Joann put a teaspoon into her mouth with a small amount of refreshing ice cream and looked at the sea in a moment of thought. She tried to guess its colour. Now that the cloudless sky was reflected in it, she would describe it as pacific blue. She thought it would be nice to one day come here with Garrett, tired of shopping on a beautiful hot day. But she quickly dismissed the thought, considering it too forward-looking. She tried to guess what he was so busy with that he couldn't accept the invitation to dinner.

"This was what I needed. I drink lots of coffee every day,"

said Jessica. She looked cheerful and it was evident that she was in a very good mood. Her beauty was dazzling and the main asset were full extremely attractive, perfectly balanced lips. She had peach complexion with golden undertone that radiated a healthy glow, and naturally modelled cheekbones. She had a sharp, slightly cool look in her caramel-brown eyes. Her English was perfect. She was born in this country into a family of emigrants of an Italian actress and a Korean doctor, who received asylum due to persecution for political beliefs. The family was doing well and growing up Jessica had everything she needed. However she didn't intend to follow in the footstep of her parents, strongly believing she could achieve more in her life and get into the higher society.

"Are you staying here long?" Joann asked.

"I don't know yet. Couple of days, maybe longer." Her voice accentuated the riddle and the mystery, and Joann thought it suited her personality. "Actually I could only book the room until Thursday as it is already booked for the next three weeks after, and there is no other room available. So I was told at reception."

"It's because of the local festival next week. We're expecting a lot of visitors."

"I will probably leave on Thursday then. That's quite sufficient for me. All I wanted was to disappear from my town for a few days before the divorce case." She paused for a moment, sipping coffee. "My husband is divorcing me," she said casually.

"I am sorry to hear that."

"That's quite alright. Right after the divorce I marry a Lord whose name I cannot reveal now. It's a secret and we don't want him to be associated with my person before the divorce," she quickly explained. "Of course, my husband is sure that I am having an affair, but he cannot prove anything. Recently he even sent his men to follow me. That's why I decided to leave for a while."

"It is very reasonable," said Joann, though there were conflicting thoughts in her mind. "I am sure you will be very happy with your new husband."

"We will certainly be happy. He cannot wait to marry me. He is mortally in love with me and filthy rich. His house is bigger than your Castle. Poor, sweet Edgar with his golf club cannot even compare with him."

"That's wonderful, how lucky you are," said Joann, thinking that it was the right thing to say and recognising Jessica was very modern.

"Well, he is old. He's almost forty years older," she said with a slight regret in her voice.

"It probably doesn't matter. The most important thing is to be happy."

"Exactly, and I know I will be incredibly happy with him," she said with exasperation. "We will go on a wedding trip to Egypt and we will spend the winter in his residence on the French Riviera. But it would be nice to keep in touch with you and Edgar. Who knows, I might pop round for a visit next summer. It is such a nice little place." She looked at her watch hastily, as if remembering she had some meeting.

Jessica seemed to Joann to be a very strange, extravagant and sometimes shocking person, but she talked to her freely and Joann found her to be quite nice. They parted in front of the store and she walked home. It was still crowded. A group of children ran around laughing and screaming. A toddler ran into her and she had to hold him up lest he fell. She walked and thought about yesterday afternoon, remembering that Garrett was different for her. He was kind but more distant and at times indifferent. He was overworked yesterday, she reasoned, and yet this change in his behaviour still troubled her.

In the afternoon, she went out with her mother for a walk and they spent an hour together chatting, but they didn't talk about the past anymore. Later on her mother was going to tea with one of her good old friends, which put her in a great mood, and Joann was very pleased. She had a plan for this afternoon and as soon as she was alone in the house she went upstairs to the left wing. The rooms in here had not been inhabited for years, but they were regularly cleaned and there was not even a bit of dust. She entered the small study, went to the window, opened the shutters and threw the panes wide. The room filled with bright sunlight and warm air. To her right, against the wall, stood two armchairs and a round table with a large lamp with a floral-patterned, fringed lampshade. Opposite were two tall bookcases and a small desk with shelves above it filled with her father's journals. She put them on the desk and sat down on the soft velveteen chair. When she opened the hard cover, she saw a dried flower of the poppy field. Memories of her childhood came flooding into her head. She remembered how, running through the fields of golden cereals, she picked the flower and how she then put it in her father's diary to remind him of her. Its colour was faded and when she took it in her hands, it crumbled in her fingers and the memory disappeared. She was leafing through the pages, not really knowing what to look for. Her father had had a large jewellery store that he sold just before his death, but there was no trace of any investments made and he didn't pay off any of the mortgages. There was no record of what he did with the money. Resigned she entered her parents` old bedroom looking around. The wardrobes and closet were empty now. The only place were father's belongings could be kept was the attic.

The attic was a dark, neglected room cluttered with old, useless furniture, children toys, picture frames and large mirror on the floor against the chimney wall. She found her father's things in a dark large trunk. She lifted his coat and a silver cigarette case fell out of it hitting loudly the wooden floorboards, apparently his things were hastily packed here and no one looked at them afterwards. She went through the clothes, looking for any clues, a note or a map with what happened to the money. At the bottom was his favourite green smoking jacket of velvet and silk. She noticed a small box in the pocket, took it out and curiously opened the lid. Inside was a luxury elegant butterfly brooch in gold with precious stones. The subtle beauty of the unexpected find delighted her. She placed the brooch in her open hand feeling its weight.

"Rubies, red and pink diamond", she judged unmistakably the type of gemstones. There was a note in the box, written in her father's hand, saying: *"For my wife, the only woman I've ever loved"*.

She was touched realizing it was a gift for her mother. A gift she never got. A small thing with a significant meaning. There was no date and it was impossible to tell when it was written, but it could mean that her father's affair had been over. Joann considered whether she should give it to her mother fearing that strong emotions would drain her shattered nerves. On the other hand, there was a chance that it would bring her peace and closure. Despite her doubts, she went to her bedroom and put the box on the table beside her mother's bed.

# 10

**S**unday **was also** hot and she spent the morning in the garden on the sun-bed, reading her father's notes, yet the flood of thoughts distracted her. She put the logs aside and decided to go for a walk and pop into the hotel. She walked in through the back door into a small hall just outside the office. After a walk in full sun, she was relieved to be in the Castle where the thick stone walls gave a slight chill, bringing immediate relief from the heat.

The office door was locked. She turned left and walked down a long narrow corridor to the reception. As she passed, she noticed a woman in the hotel foyer, and to her surprise she recognised it was Louise. It angered her. She couldn't believe that she dared to show up here after the last time they spoke. She walked over as Louise turned to her, and she saw the lost look in her eyes. It surprised her again because she expected Louise might be feisty and nonchalant. Instead she was very calm. She had the sweet disarming appearance with the big blue eyes, bright red lips and blonde curls. In the cinched waistline dress fitted to the hips, short puff sleeves and excellent, flawless makeup she looked like a Hollywood star on the silver screen. Like she was cut from a journal.

"Jo," she said with a soft, pleading voice. It looked like she was afraid the unexpected meeting with Joann would end in conflict again, and she wanted to reconcile with her.

"I asked you not to come here." Joann moved closer to her.

"That's okay." She recognised Garrett's voice behind her and was surprised by his sudden appearance. "Louise is with me." He joined them. "She's my guest, I invited her."

Joann did not respond, instead she looked at him with wide, astonished eyes, and felt something freeze in her. At that moment, she could not forgive him these words and understood that this was the reason why he couldn't accept the invitation to dinner. It was because he had a date with Louise. Hurt and disappointed, she turned without saying anything and walked away.

* * *

Louise looked at Garrett uncertainly. "Do you think it's a good idea to have dinner here?"

"Yes, I very much think so. People have to get used to seeing us together," he said confidently.

They sat down at a square table covered with a white cloth. He watched her while she looked at the menu. Someone who knew him might have noticed that something changed in his gaze. There was now more hope and optimism in that look. But for her it was simply the gentle look of someone she found to be a pleasant man.

They placed their order and looked into each other's eyes

for a moment in silence. He would have given a lot to find out what she was thinking. He was almost one-hundred percent sure that she was the woman. He knew it from the moment he first saw her here at the hotel bar only two days ago. She awakened his suppressed feelings and he promised himself that he would do anything not to spoil it this time.

\* \* \*

Joann entered the house and silently slipped upstairs to her bedroom, not wanting to see anyone right now. She sat down in a large, comfortable armchair in front of the window and stared at the green crowns of the yew trees in the garden. She felt deeply hurt, twice as much by the fact that he had a date with that woman and that he put her in such an awkward situation there in the hotel foyer. Her dreams were starting to fall apart and in a sudden rush of despair she couldn't see a way to fix it. Now she remembered her mother's words when she said Louise had come back for revenge, and if so then the revenge was successful indeed. Taking away the man with whom Joann planned to make a life for herself was the best revenge one could imagine.

This thought was devastating and she couldn't yet recover. It suddenly occurred to her that he was just making a terrible mistake. That he had been seduced by her unusual beauty and acquired grace. Joann was sure that as soon as he got to know her better, found out all the truth about her, he would understand how terribly wrong he was in choosing her. She knew Louise was an abandoned child with no father, no family, no education and no profession and she'd learned from some friends that she was now divorced. She decided she would speak to him, hoping to talk some sense into him. She believed that he would shake off this blindness and break with Louise.

## 11

When Joann entered the office the next morning Garrett was already there. He stood facing the window and turned as he heard footsteps. She put her purse down on the desk but didn't sit. She was prepared for this conversation and yet she felt nervous.

"Yesterday," he started.

"You are making a mistake dating that woman," she interrupted. She was angry with him and wanted to shout in his face, but instead she spoke in a slightly choppy voice. "She is bad. My brother died because of her and if my mum sees her here…"

He came close and put his hand on her shoulder. She knew that it was only a friendly gesture to comfort her and it meant nothing more than that. She was losing him and it scared her.

"She is nothing but an abandoned orphan looking for rich men," she said abruptly. She saw a sad, worried look in his eyes.

"I don't care who she is," he said with a mild voice. "I'm only sorry that you feel that way about her. You and Louise could get on well together if you just tried."

These words were unacceptable to her and she looked for the appropriate denial.

"FIRE! FIRE!" a man screamed from outside the office.

They looked at each other for a fraction of a second with confused eyes, and in the tension caused by the scream, both ran out into the corridor. Smoke was coming from one of the two parlours and they ran towards it. Joann saw the newspaper rack burning and the fire had reached the carpet and the leather sofa. Alfred and Ben were trying to kill the flames with thick curtains they'd torn from the windows and two chefs ran over with buckets of water.

"Extinguisher!" she shouted. In a rush of adrenaline, she ran to the hall and came back carrying the extinguisher. Garrett took it from her hands and sprayed the flames. Thanks to the joint effort, the fire slowly went out, leaving charred areas. The room was full of smoke and they opened all windows. Thankfully breakfast was nearly over and most of the guests were out. A few of them stood there watching and she calmed them by saying that everything was under control now.

Garrett patted Alfred on the shoulder, thanked him, Ben and the others and said that they did a good job. The fire truck arrived, alerted by the receptionist. They examined the parlour and said that it looked like an accident caused by a cigarette butt which had fallen into the newspaper rack from a standing ashtray.

Garrett walked over to Ben who was staring at the damage. "Have you finished upstairs, Ben?"

"Just about," he answered politely.

"Will you be able to sort out this mess here?"

"Yes, I will. It will take me a couple of days."

"Good and, Ben, I want to hire you full time."

"Thank you, sir." Ben bowed slightly.

"That's okay. Bring your papers down to my office tomorrow and I'll sort it for you."

Joann and Garrett went out into the little courtyard to take a fresh breath. The day was not so hot, but it was pleasantly warm. There were a few round iron tables with chairs outside, but they didn't sit down. The fresh air had a soothing effect and Joann managed to get hold of her nerves.

"That was close," said Garrett. "Do you think it was an accident?"

She noticed there was doubt in his voice. "Yes. Of course," she replied confidently. "Do you have any doubts?"

"I don't know. Someone might have done it on purpose, although I can't find a reason why. I just have a strange feeling it was not an accident."

"I don't think so. Anyway, no more standing ashtrays. We have to replace them with the usual table ones. Lesson learned."

Edgar emerged through a narrow passage surrounded on both sides by a stone fence overgrown with ivy and jasmine branches and walked up to them. "I heard there was a fire." He paused. "But why I am not surprised. It looks like I was right all along. You two just can't take your eyes off each other." He smiled wickedly.

Garrett trembled at his words, walked over to Edgar and whispered something in his ear. Joann didn't hear what it was. As they exchanged a few more words with each other, she left them and went inside.

It occurred to her that Edgar never comes to the hotel in the morning and that it was strange that he came here at this time today, just after the fire. She began to wonder if Garrett's suspicions may be true. She felt uneasy. Had the trust she placed in Edgar betrayed her? Would an old acquaintance and friend of the family conspire against her and go so far as to set fire to the hotel. She quickly dismissed that thought. Once again, she trusted her intuition that told her that he wasn't bad. She assumed it was Louise who had something to do with it and decided to share this suspicion with Garrett. She hoped that he would finally believe her and see through Louise.

"Jo," the receptionist called when she spotted her in the hall. "You have a phone call from Mildred. She's calling from the house."

Joann picked up the receiver. As she talked to Mildred her stress began to build again. "I'll be right back," she said to her and hung up the phone. She caught up with Garrett in the hall. "I have to go home."

"Is everything alright?" he asked watching her with concern.

"There's something wrong with my mother. Mildred has just phoned."

"You have to go then. Don't rush back. I'll take care of everything here and let me know if you need anything."

# 12

*J*oann entered the house and Mildred met her downstairs in the hall. She told Joann that her mother was acting weird, talking to someone who wasn't there, and Mildred got scared. Joann started to worry. Suddenly she heard the elderly woman upstairs, screaming loudly. With a trembling heart she ran there. Her mother opened a double door to the left wing that was once her and her husband's bedroom, though the wing was not in use now.

"I FORGIVE YOU!" she shouted, entering the small hall. "I FORGIVE YOU!" She opened both sides of another double door to a small study, went across the room and through another double door to a large bedroom. "I forgive you, Henry!" She put her hands up. "I release you!" She opened a French balcony door and leaned against the railing, facing the garden. "Henry! Henry!"

Joann ran up to her but her mother was in a trance and her eyes didn't take in her surroundings. Jo embraced her.

"Let me go, let me go." She tried to break free and started to cry.

"It's me. Mum, it's Joann. Let's go out of here. We have to go now. Let's go."

A flash of consciousness appeared in the woman's eyes and Jo led her out of the room. She looked exhausted and lacking any strength. Joann led her to her bedroom, put her to bed and phoned the doctor.

Still quivering, she went downstairs to the living room and sat in the armchair with a glass of wine. Her mind was racing. She wondered if there could be any spiritual presence in the house that she was unable to see. Was it possible that her father's spirit had appeared to her mother? Or maybe it had been Richard. Neither of them died in the house. Her father died at the scene of the accident and Richard in the hospital. And why would he start to appear now after so many years? Joann doubted it. She has never seen any ghosts and didn't really believe in them. She had to face the fact that her mother's illness had progressed dramatically and the current medications were no longer working. The only hope she had was a doctor, whom she was now waiting patiently for.

She stroked the dog who sat down next to her and put his head on her lap. She stared out at the garden through the large patio door in front of her, noticing with regret how different it was from Louise's cottage garden with the countless amounts of flowers, shrubs, climbers and roses. Her own garden was plain, with short cut grass, neatly trimmed yew trees and barberries. She always kept her garden simple, easy to maintain, but did it make it characterless. Not even one single rose bush in there. A rose, that fragrance of which she couldn't describe though some people called it divine. A fragrance that was intoxicating and incapacitating, and the other day had made her feel weak, depriving her of her impulse to fight. Roses that guarded the little cottage and its beautiful owner against intruders.

She thought how much different Louise and her were. Totally different personalities, like north and south poles. And she realised that when Garrett chose Louise over her, he could have not possibly made a mistake, because the difference between them was too obvious.

\* \* \*

Doctor Henderson was an older, kind man and very respected. He had lived all his life in this town and started his career here as a young doctor. He assisted her mother in childbirth and when Joann was little he used to joke that he was the first person to welcome her into this world. She made him a cup of tea and they sat at a table.

"I'm concerned about your mother's mental health. I'm afraid there's not much I can prescribe. When was the last time she went on holiday?" he asked.

"Years ago. She doesn't like to leave the house for too long."

"I'm thinking of changing the scenery, sending her to a rest bay for a while. Not far from here, by the sea, with twenty-four-hour nurse care, and you can visit her there at any time," he said in a sincere, friendly voice.

"It's worth trying, thank you, doctor," she replied with hope in her voice.

"Good. I'll phone them and let them know that you are bringing her today. Don't be so worried. I'm sure it will do her good. I would advise you to take a break and go some-where nice for a couple of days. You need some rest, too," he said and tapped a finger on her hand as if she was still the same little girl from years ago.

# 13

*T*hat evening was busy at the hotel and all lights were on. The local festival and nice weather drew a lot of people in and the town was bursting at the seams. The Castle's bar, parlour and outdoor courtyard tables were full of hotel guests and locals. They ordered drinks and chatted loudly. Quite a few people turned up for dinner and the restaurant served until late. Garrett decided to join them too. He answered some questions about the fire and reassured everybody that it was an accident and nothing to worry about. There was a nice mood and people seemed relaxed. The service did their best to please them and everybody seemed to be having a nice time. It got late quickly.

It was a long day for Garrett and he was tired when he got home. He parked in front of the house. It was already dark. Lights in nearby houses shone. The night grew colder and the air was brisk. It was a full moon. He looked up the sky. The moon shone in all its splendour. The street was nearly empty. Two men were walking on the pavement. Garrett started towards the house, when suddenly they lunged at him from behind with wooden sticks. One of them hit his head and his hat fell to the ground. He fought back but felt his knees buckle under him and he saw a bright light approaching. Suddenly the attack stopped and they ran away. He heard an engine and the headlights of a car came closer, blinding him.

When he opened his eyes again, he was in bed, in a small, white room with a dim light. A young woman in a white coat told him that he was lucky and to sleep now.

* * *

Joann took her mother to the rest bay house and stayed with her overnight in the guest room. She said goodbye to her the next morning and came back home by taxi. It was noon when she arrived at the hospital. Garrett was sitting up in bed, leaning against pillows. He had a bruise around his eye that looked sore.

"I found out about the attack from Inspector Hawkins. He phoned me and asked if I suspected anyone," she said. "How are you feeling?" She sat down on a chair by his bedside.

"Not that bad. I'm going back to work tomorrow," he said and added "It was Edgar".

"Edgar?"

"Yes, Edgar saved my life. He was driving by on his way home from the golf club."

"Thank God he was driving there then," she commented feeling grateful to Edgar. "Don't you think the attack might have something to do with Louise?"

"Louise? Nonsense," he huffed. "What's on your mind?

The inspector suggested it was a robbery."

Joann walked over to the small window then turned back to face him. "I know you won't like what I have to say, but strange things have started happening here since she came back. I am sure she's behind all this and I am going to report it to the police." She waited expectantly for his answer.

He was silent for a while and she realised her words seemed absurd to him. That he had no doubts about Louise whatsoever, and was only concerned about the conflict between the women. Her suspicions were reinforced when he said calmly, "Louise is not that type of person. She would never do anything bad, even if she had a reason, even if she hated me or anybody else. I don't support this quarrel between you. I don't want to take anybody's side or have a disagreement with my partners. It's not good for business. I'm in favour of reconciling old quarrels, although they are still painful. Perhaps I could talk to your mother and try to charm her."

He winked at her and smiled, but in a moment he got serious again. "Or we could find ways for Louise and your mother to avoid each other. I would not dare to upset your mother, but I also don't want to hurt Louise's feelings and forbid her from coming to the Castle, now or when she becomes my wife."

The word 'wife' stung her, and she felt a pang in her heart. It sounded very definitive and Joann knew there was nothing else to add that would change his mind about her. Of course, she realised that everything he'd said was sensible. They had to maintain a good atmosphere in order for the business to run smoothly and bring in a profit. Things would have to change, she would have to change, to adapt to the new reality. There was no more room here for an old grudge that was never truly justified, and she understood that well, his message was clear, but she didn't have to accept it.

On her way back to the Castle, she couldn't help feeling angry with Louise again. Something inside her was hounding her to revolt and fight for him. She caught herself thinking that it would be better if something happened to make him hate Louise. She felt defeated and it didn't feel good.

She entered the hotel very energetically, carried away by anxiety and anger.

"A gentleman is waiting for you in the parlour," she heard Connie say, but she didn't care about it and didn't stop. She went through the hall with quick steps straight to the office. She didn't want to know about anything at the moment. She wanted to be alone, clear her head and calm down.

After a few minutes, she heard knocking. The door opened and, without waiting for an invitation, a man entered the room. He was about her age, well dressed, with dark blonde hair and a big smile on his face. He didn't look to her like a policeman sent to ask questions about the attack. She looked at him curiously.

"I'm Jeff Fereday, Garrett's younger brother," he introduced himself. "I visited him in the hospital this morning and already managed to have a look around the town." He reached out to greet her. "It looks like he's going to be alright, old boy."

Joann was totally surprised and embarrassed that she hadn't thought to notify Garrett's family about the attack, but somebody had. Probably the police.

"Garrett never told me about you coming," she said, staring at him in confusion.

"That's Garrett. He never told me that his business partner was such a beautiful lady. Like lady Godiva," he said, and she burst out laughing at being compared to a naked woman riding a horse through the middle of town. It was the first time in a long time she'd laughed spontaneously, let go of her tension and relaxed for a moment. He also laughed and it was evident that he was happy with his joke.

"I came to meet you and invite you for dinner tonight, hoping that you would accept." He stopped and looked at her for a moment in silence. "But now I think it might be a better idea to invite you to the theatre, too."

"Theatre?"

"Yes, tonight."

"Tonight?" she repeated loudly.

"Why not? I guess the Castle will still be standing here tomorrow, but the play has one last showing tonight."

She figured he was right about it, and thought it was exactly what she needed, to get away from her problems and for a moment forget about stressful life. She knew she shouldn't, she didn't know Jeff at all, but she was reassured that he was Gareth's brother and she trusted in his good manners.

"Are we going to get the tickets then?" she rejoiced at the thought of a nice evening.

"Well, miraculously, I already have two." He took them out of his pocket, raised them up and shook them a few times, smiling. He was nice, funny and like a breath of fresh air shook all the troubles off her shoulder in seconds.

Jeff was the youngest in the Fereday family. As a child

he received lots of care and attention from the female half of the family and growing up surrounded by women, he thought he understood them well. He looked like a man with a sunny disposition and a great deal of optimism and Joann picked up on his good mood.

# 14

The evening spent in Jeff's company was pleasant. They talked a lot but he spoke the most. The show turned out to be a comedy and they both enjoyed it, laughing and clapping. By the time they left the theatre it was getting dark.

"I know that I am unbearable for having taken your whole evening, but I would like to ask you for one more thing," he said, looking her in the eyes.

"What do you want to ask me for?"

"Let's go for a walk on the beach. There is no wind, the moon is full and it will be wonderful," he said enthusiastically.

"I don't think I've ever been on the beach at this time."

"Me neither. But I dreamed that. I dreamed of taking a walk with a beautiful woman on the seashore by the light of the full moon. She would be in a long evening gown, me in a tuxedo. These will be memories that we will never forget." He looked at her and with such sincerity that she wanted this romantic trip to the seafront too.

They drove to a wild beach outside the town. There were no buildings or lights there but the big, round moon shone silver and made the night bright. The beach was large, wide and sandy, surrounded by dunes overgrown with swaying beach grass and gorse. The waves were small and lapped gently against the shore. The hot air smelt of ocean, slowly cooling down in the evening chill. She slightly lifted her dress in her hand, walking barefoot on the sand. He held his shoes by their tied laces and the legs of his trousers were rolled up. They were silent for a while, gazing at the stars. She let her hair down and enjoyed the sea breeze blowing in her face. She closed her eyes to listen to the waves and breathe the scent of the night, it smelt like perfume with corals and amber. She was completely relaxed. Right now, she didn't want the walk to end.

"I have to take you sailing sometime," he said breaking the silence, staring at the silver glow of the moon reflecting in the water.

"Do you sail?" she asked.

"Yes, the London boy you are looking at can sail quite well," he said with a smile. "I rented a sailing boat for tomorrow morning. I hope there will be a little more wind. What are you doing tomorrow?"

"The doctor left Garrett in the hospital for another day or two, so tomorrow I'll have to be in the hotel taking care of everything. After work I was going to visit my mother in the rest bay."

"Alright." He thought for a short while. "My plan is this. In the morning I will go sailing for a couple of hours, then I will pick up Garrett from the hospital and in the afternoon, I will take you to your mother. How does that sound?"

"It sounds good to me," she said happily, and then she ran along the shore and Jeff followed her, laughing.

\* \* \*

He drove her home late at night, but in the morning, she got up early after just a few hours of sleep and was in a great mood. She let the dogs out into the garden and they sniffed around excitedly. When she looked at the ground, she noticed a large man's shoe print right next to the patio. It looked fresh. Someone must have been walking on her property last night.

She looked around the house, but found no other traces and hoped it must have been a stranger who got lost or was looking for a shortcut. She left the dogs outside and hurried to work. Garrett was leaving the hospital today but the doctor told him not go to work until tomorrow, and even though he insisted on coming when they spoke over the phone, Joann told him that he should rest.

The hotel was noisy. Guests were going out to the beach with towels, and the small children ran happily. The burned furniture in the parlour had already been taken out and the old ruined carpeting had been removed. Ben was painting the walls to get rid of the burning smell. The day passed quickly but calmly enough. Jeff picked her up in the late afternoon. Outside the town, the road partly ran through the forest and picturesque fields over which small white clouds were suspended in a row, looking like little lambs following one another. They enjoyed the tour and the company of each other, having the impression of getting along pretty well.

"I was thinking today while sailing," Jeff began.

"What about?"

"I noted that the marina in the bay can barely contain all the boats," he said, speaking with a lively tone.

"Yes, it was built a long time ago." She looked at him, expecting him to tell her something interesting as usual.

"Exactly. Now more people can afford to buy a sailing boat and boats are more modern and bigger. This marina is simply too small. I noticed while sailing that right next to it is quite a convenient spot, naturally adapted for the marina. Investing some money in it, you could do good business with a quick return."

"Then you could come here more often."

"Or I could stay here."

"Does that mean you are considering living here?" she asked happily, unable to hide her excitement.

"I consider this possibility very seriously." He smiled at the sight of her wide-open, surprised eyes. "I would have a brother here. If he dared to make his dreams come true, maybe I can do it too."

Jeff dropped her off in front of the main entrance to the rest bay and went to refuel. Joann went to see her mother and found her walking slowly in the company of a few people about her age. They were returning from a walk by the sea. Joann joined them and took her mother by the arm. They walked through the garden to the terrace of the large house standing on a small hill. She turned to look at the beautiful sight. Behind them, a dozen or so metres away, was the sea. The waves moved, humming softly and shimmering in the rays of the sun that was already quite low on the horizon.

"I'm glad you found company here," said Joann. They slowed down and stayed a little bit behind.

"I met a few nice people here."

"That's really good, Mum."

"Especially Graham. He's a widower like me and we talk to each other a lot. He has such an understanding view of life. He says we can only be happy now in the present. If we stick to the past, we may never be happy again. I think I can finally think of your father and not feel angry or sad."

"You were happy with him," said Joann.

"Yes, I was. My first husband was sickly, he couldn't have children. When he died, I met Henry. He had a jewellery store, so he could provide for a family. And I wanted so much to have a family and children. I thought this was my second chance. Henry cared for us and was a good father."

"Did he tell you what he did with the money after selling the store?"

"No. I trusted him completely on financial matters. He was healthy, he didn't expect sudden death. He did not tell me anything about it." She walked in silence for a while. "What about the Castle? How is Garrett, our new business partner?" She changed the subject.

"I am afraid you need to find out about something." Joann paused and took a deep breath. "It's very likely that Garrett and Louise will get engaged."

Her mother stared blankly somewhere ahead and was silent for a moment that seemed too long to Joann. Then, without interrupting her walk, she said, "I don't think anything can surprise me anymore. I'm already reconciled with everything," she said in a calm, indifferent voice.

Jeff returned and he found them in the garden.

"Mum," said Joann happy to see him, secretly hopping she would approve of him, "this is Jeff Fereday, Garrett's younger brother."

"Oh my God!" She stared at him with bewildered eyes. "He looks just like my dear Richard. The same radiant look and smile. "You must tell me about yourself, young man," she said to him and, infatuated with his person, took him by the arm and walked with him towards the terrace.

# 15

*J*oann and Jeff came back in the evening and made a date for the next day. She went to the garden to call the dogs and walked with them for a while. With a smile on her face, she pondered the nice day they had spent today. Jeff was fun and a delight to be with. She excitedly wondered where he would take her tomorrow and she hoped to go sailing. A day at sea would be a relaxing adventure in great company.

The dogs ran among the trees and kept barking at a squirrel on the large oak. It was starting to turn grey and Joann felt tired.

She noticed something on the ground and casually walked over to see what it was. With concern, she realised it was two cigarette butts under the large overgrown barberry bush. So, someone had been on her property last night, standing here, unnoticed as they watched the house. She turned abruptly when something rustled behind her, but no one was there and the dogs were calm. She called them close and looked around fearfully before returning home, where she locked the door and closed all the shutters.

It was dark in the house and she turned on the lights.

Various thoughts came to her mind and she began to put them all together. She realised now that there was no spirit in the house, that they were haunted by a living man of flesh and blood who left a shoe print and cigarette butts. But she couldn't guess who it was or what he wanted. Did he want to kill them? She didn't know whether to call the police, and decided to talk to the inspector tomorrow morning.

She took out the prepared dinner from the refrigerator, but thoughts troubled her and she could not eat. She was already very tired and went upstairs to her bedroom, bolting the door from the inside. She stayed awake all night, sitting on the bed and covered by the quilt. She froze when she heard a strange sound inside the house. If it was a stranger, the dogs would start barking. After a while, she realised the noise had been one of the dogs coming to her bedroom door, sniffing at it and then going back downstairs. Joann calmed herself, got up, stretched to the window and slightly opened the shutters.

It was completely dark outside, but she noticed a tiny glowing spot in the darkness of the garden. The spot looked like the bulb of a lit cigarette. It lit up for a short while and then went out. The man had returned and was only a few metres from the house. Panic took hold of her. She could sneak downstairs to the phone and call for help. She listened carefully, holding her breath. It was very quiet in the house now and the dogs downstairs showed no sign of anxiety.

After a while, she wasn't sure anymore if she had actually seen the lit cigarette or if it was only her imagination. She thought she heard an engine motor in front of the house, but from her bedroom window she could not see what was happening on that side. Then there was a thud against the front door. Her heart quivered. The dogs rushed to the door, barking furiously. She had to find out who it was. Joann left her bedroom and stood at the top of the stairs looking down the hall at the front door, ready to head back to her bedroom and bolt the door. The banging on the door was repeated, much louder.

"Jo! Open the door." She heard a low male voice. "It's me, Edgar."

She hesitated, then ran downstairs to the front door. Now she thought she heard a woman's voice behind him, too. She turned on the hall light and opened the door ajar. Cool air blew in.

"Thank God you opened. What took you so long?" he asked impatiently, as if receiving guests in the middle of the night was a normal thing. She looked at his face. He wasn't drunk but one could see he'd had a drink or two that night. She heard a car door slam shut and footsteps approaching.

"After you," said a woman's lofty voice.

"After you, madam," replied an irritated female voice. Soon, two women approached the door. Lucy and Jessica Brixton.

"Hello, my dear," said Jessica.

"Hello, Jo," Lucy said hesitantly.

They all came inside and settled on the comfy sofas in the living room. Joann was completely surprised and at the same time felt relieved that she was no longer alone and that her nightmare was over.

"Is your service awake? I want hot chocolate," said Jessica.

"There is no service in this house, you have to make it

yourself, Jess," said Edgar.

"I'll get it for you." Joann stood up.

"Better make me a proper drink then, gin and tonic."

"I will do it," said Edgar, walking over to the trolley with alcohol. "Jo, Lucy, what will you drink?"

"Same for me," said Lucy.

"A glass of port, please," said Joann. She sat impatiently, waiting for an explanation for this sudden, late-night arrival, guessing that this was not an ordinary courtesy visit. There was a momentary silence. Edgar rang the bottles and poured drinks.

Joann looked at him and the women around him, glad she was right about him all along. Now she could clearly see his true nature. His superficial feelings, inability to commit to a serious relationship, instead constantly flirting with women in a drunken stupor. She felt strong dislike for Edgar and was content not to be with him. If she ever had any feelings for him, they were over now. She was relived to finally move on and letting go of the past, feeling like a new person. She thought about Jeff and how lucky she was to have him around.

"Darling," Jessica said to Joann, "I have to stay at your house for the night." She took a cigarette holder out of her purse, put a cigarette in and lit it.

"Jessica came to us at the bowling club tonight," Edgar explained and serving the drinks. "We had a competition and there were a few journalists. One of them kept looking at Jess and we think he recognised her because he tried to take a picture of her. We had to escape from there through the back door."

"He wouldn't have recognised her if she hadn't offended me and attracted everyone's attention," said Lucy in phlegmatic, slightly indignant tone. She was passionate about Edgar and wanted to show him, she wouldn't let anyone treat her badly. She was sitting on the edge of the armchair with a glass in hand. Jessica ignored her comment without even looking at her.

"I have to avoid any scandals at the moment," she said. "You understand, my dear, that I cannot show up at the hotel now, because journalists will be waiting for me there."

"We all need to avoid scandals," Lucy interrupted looking at Edgar, seeking support in his gaze.

"I will sleep here tonight and leave in the early morning before they find me here," said Jessica and puffed on her cigarette.

"It will be a bigger scandal if you crash your car under the influence of alcohol," Lucy said in that calm, firm tone of hers. "If I were you, I wouldn't drink anymore tonight since you're planning on driving in the morning."

"Accept that you will never be me, my dear. I am the wife of a world-famous film producer," Jessica said haughtily.

"Of course, Jessica, I will be pleased. The guest room is always ready." Joann smiled at her. Then she remembered the stranger in the garden and turned to Edgar. "Were you in the garden a few moments ago?"

"Me? No. What for?"

"I saw a cigarette lit under the trees in front of the house. Someone was standing there, hidden in the trees."

"You don't mean to say that journalists have already found out that I am here?" asked Jessica anxiously.

"No. It was before you came."

"What's going on here?" said Edgar. "It was such a quiet town. Nothing ever happened here. I'll go and check it out." He got up and went to the patio door.

"Better not go out." Joann stopped him. "It could be the same men who attacked Garrett the other night."

"I'll let the dogs out then. They will start barking if they sniff out something." He opened the door and called the dogs, patted them on the back and let them out into the garden. They ran off, disappearing into the darkness. Occasionally, they appeared for a moment and then disappeared again. It was quiet out there and the night was cold. Edgar stood in the open doorway smoking a cigarette. Cold wind blew into the living room.

"You will freeze us here, for God's sake," shouted Jessica with very little concern about what was going on. He called the dogs and let them in.

"It seems they didn't even sniff out a fox," he said. "I don't think anyone is there. Are you sure you didn't imagine it?"

"I am rather sure," she answered.

"Do you want me to stay overnight?" he asked. There was something intimate in his voice, discreetly suggesting a passionate night together. He touched her arm tenderly, looking deep into her eyes with an excited, erotic look, yet her senses didn't move. Her emotions and desires didn't arouse in her. She remained cool and composed, knowing exactly what she wanted without shadow of a doubt.

"No Edgar", she said firmly. "I'll be alright. Even if someone was there, he is probably already gone".

"Edgar has to bring me home tonight," Lucy interrupted.

"Lock the door and speak to the inspector tomorrow," he advised her.

Lucy and Edgar got in the car and drove away. Jessica's car was left in front of the house. Joann bolted the door and led the slightly tipsy Jessica into the guest bedroom. She felt fatally worn out, went to her bedroom, lay down in bed and fell asleep immediately.

In the morning, she was awakened by sounds downstairs. She looked at the clock and noticed that it was only six in the morning. It was possible that Jessica was already up. She put on a dressing gown and opened the shutters, letting a pale light fall into the room. With disappointment, she noticed that the sun was now hidden behind clouds. They had forecast rain for today. Reluctantly, she went downstairs, surprised to see Jessica dressed and ready to go.

"I was just going to wake you up to say goodbye," she said. Her lips curved into a smile that seemed warm and sincere. She put out her cigarette in the ashtray and got up from the couch. "I have to sneak through the town before the journalists wake up. They would follow me if they saw me. I know how these things work." She headed for the exit.

"Wait a moment, I'll make tea" offered Joann.

"That's alright. I had some water since your service was off. Terribly nice of you to put me up. It's a pity that we could not talk any longer."

"It is a pity. Maybe we can make up for it someday," said Joann, walking her to the car. Tiny raindrops began to fall.

"Oh, I am sure of it. Leave it with me and I will think how to organise it." Jessica got into the car.

"That would be great," said Joann. "Drive carefully."
"I hope to see you soon," she said as she drove away.

# 16

nspector Hawkins knocked on Garrett's door early in the morning with two of his men. He was an energetic man and entered the house with verve. They went to the living room and Garrett offered them a drink but they declined.

"There was a break-in at the Whitby estate last night," he said to Garrett. "Old Whitby was killed at the scene. His handmaiden was hospitalised, unconscious with serious injuries."

"That's terrible. Who did this?" Garrett was devastated by this brutal attack on a defenceless elderly man and his servant.

"We suspect fugitives from North Yorkshire prison. They escaped a few weeks ago, killing a policeman in the process. Scotland Yard has been looking for them in Yorkshire and up in Scotland, but didn't expect them to go south."

"Do you think they are here now?"

"We are still not sure if it is them. There is no one who saw them here or who could identify them. I wonder if you could. Maybe it's the same two who attacked you the other night. I have their pictures here. Can you look and see if you can recognise them?" He handed Garrett the photos.

"I won't be able to help, I didn't see their faces," said Garrett, but he took the photos and looked at them carefully. "I know this man," he exclaimed and pointed to the man in the photo.

"You recognise him? Is it one of those who attacked you?"

"This man works for us at the hotel. His name is Ben. We hired him quite recently to do some work around the hotel."

"This man is not Ben," Inspector Hawkins said. "This is Brandon Wolf, dangerous criminal. And the other one is his accomplice. Where is he now?"

"At the hotel," said Garrett.

\* \* \*

Joann came to work earlier than usual. A few people were having breakfast in the restaurant but the foyer was completely empty and quiet. She went down the narrow corridor to the office. The door wasn't locked and she thought Garrett must have come to work early too. When she went in, he wasn't there and the disordered room surprised her. Papers were on the floor and the cupboard was open. She came closer and noticed that the money box was gone. She understood what happened, but her mind refused to accept that they had been robbed.

The door closed softly behind her and Joann turned around. Ben was by the door and she didn't understand why he was here. There was a large hammer in his hand and he put it to his lips.

"Shush, don't open your mouth," he said. His face looked different now, sinister, hate gleaming in his eyes. She realised now what had happened. She must have surprised him during the robbery. "Now I will pay you back, for your family putting me in jail for stealing your father's wallet, back on the Irish coast years ago.," he said with a mocking smile. "You didn't recognise me, did you? Far too caught up in your own spoiled existence. I've been looking for you. It took me a long time, but I always knew I would find you, get a revenge and pay. Where is the treasure? I came to claim it. Where is it?" he asked with anger but she had no idea what treasure he was talking about.

"Where is the treasure?" He repeated. "Talk!"

"I don't know, I don't know" she said horrified.

"I remember you smiled ironically then. You are the same as your father. He stared down at me as they locked me up." He moved towards her and his fierce expression frightened her. Fear paralysed her and she couldn't speak as she watched him approach.

"I have been watching you all the time since I arrived here, waiting for the opportunity to stop that smile." He continued towards her slowly, as if he was enjoying her agony.

She stepped back and clung to the cupboard behind her, seeing no chance of rescue. He would hit her in a moment and she wouldn't be able to do anything to save herself. He stood in front of her and with a quick movement raised the hammer up. Joann screamed and covered her head with her hands. At the same time, he backed away fast, as if something had scared him or pushed him away, and his face paled.

He backed up further, raising his hands and covering his head.

"NO, YOU CAN'T DO ANYTHING TO ME," he exclaimed. "YOU ARE DEAD. GO AWAY."

He stepped back and hit the empty space in front of him. He dropped the hammer and grabbed his neck choking, desperate to catch a breath as his eyes grew enormous and terrified.

Someone knocked and opened the door.

"Are you alright, Jo?" the maid stood in the doorway. "I heard screaming."

Ben pushed her away and ran out through the back door.

* * *

When Garrett and Inspector Hawkins entered the office, Joann was sitting on the sofa. Maid Clovis brought her a glass of brandy to help her recover from the shock. She was still shaking.

"We just found out what happened," Garrett said. "Inspector Hawkins has sent his men to search for him." He walked over and sat on the couch.

The inspector bent down and picked up the hammer still lying on the floor.

"He tried to hit me with that," she said. "But he suddenly stopped as if something scared him off or he went mad."

"How much money was in the box?" asked the inspector. He pulled a chair next to the sofa and sat down.

"One week's income. He seemed to be looking for

something else too but I don't know what", she said. "I suppose he stole the silver candlesticks too. I suspected a few people, but not him."

"He set the fire in the parlour too, and then attacked Garrett the other night," the inspector said.

"Why did he do it?" she asked.

"Because his job here was coming to the end," explained Garrett. "Renovating the parlour after the fire gave him the time he needed to stay here, to walk around without arousing suspicions, and to prepare for the robbery. When I told him I wanted to hire him full time and asked him to bring me his papers, he got scared that I would suspect something if he didn't bring them, so he tried to get rid of me," he finished and everything he said made sense to her now.

"Did he say anything significant?" asked the inspector.

"I don't know. All he said was that he wanted revenge. Apparently, my father put him in jail for stealing his wallet years ago." She burst into tears at the memory of the awful moments a few minutes ago but quickly regained her composure.

"Let me know if you remember anything else. I have to see to the chase and make sure we have secured all the escape routes, otherwise they will be far away from here in a couple of hours." Inspector Hawkins stood up and left via the back door.

"Are you feeling any better?" Garrett asked in a concerned voice. "Maybe you should stay home and rest today."

"No, I don't want to go home. I can work, I'm alright."

"No, you are not. You are shaking."

"I know where to take her," Jeff said, entering the room.

He had a devastated expression on his face when he saw her distraught. He wanted to console her immediately, he walked over and took her hand. Joann looked at him with eyes still wet from tears. "Let's go on a boat. Let's go sailing." His soft voice and the warm touch of his hands comforted her, and she managed to smile.

# 17

*J*oann jumped into sports trousers and flat shoes. She knew the basics of sailing and the idea of going to sea with Jeff excited her, although the stress of the attack had not yet left her.

When they arrived, the rain had just stopped and it was quiet and peaceful in the marina. There were a few walkers admiring the surroundings and small stone houses situated only a dozen metres from the shore. The wind was blowing and boats moored at the quay swayed slightly in the water. The sky was covered with white clouds that flowed with gusts of wind. Here and there the rays of the sun pierced through. Seagulls scuttled across the sky and cried loudly. A unique sea scent rose from the waves and carried in the air. It was a scent that reminded her of shells, seaweed and the taste of salt. She realised that she hadn't been here for months and she was glad she came back before the end of summer. They went out to sea by sailing boat with a small cabin, rented by Jeff. He turned out to be quite a good sailor. The yacht picked up speed quickly and soon they were out on the high seas. The cry of the seagulls was no longer heard. It was quite and calm. The waves hummed. The wind rustled in the rigging.

She stared at the waves and thought back to the moment when she had come face to face with death. She felt helpless and terrified again. The fear was so strong it overwhelmed her, and she withdrew into herself. Jeff looked at her from time to time, clearly concerned by the absent expression on her face and knowing her mind was elsewhere. When he spoke to her she replied briefly, but after a while she didn't listen to him anymore, instead staring at the water, letting her consciousness drift away. Jeff fell silent and left her with her thoughts.

Dark clouds were quickly covering the sky and the wind intensified, tugging at her hair, but she didn't care. Lost in thought, she relived the nightmare of the early morning over and over again, trying to deal with this terrible fear.

"Reef the mainsail!" She heard a distant cry and when she looked around the sky was overcast. The wind was blowing hard, waves lapped at the yacht, tilting it, and water poured onboard. Jeff was trying to hold the helm, but it was resistant, preventing any manoeuvre of the boat and the yacht tilted more and more. Joann remembered just what to do. They had to flatten the sail, reef the mainsail and the foresail. With vigour, she set off to the sails. The wind was violent and strong, pushing her away and tearing at the sails. She struggled with them while he steered the boat.

The excitement of fighting the elements overwhelmed her and she felt a surge of strength to overcome it. She managed to reef the mainsail and then the foresail to the middle. The sense of powerlessness which had not left her from the moment of the attack ceased unexpectedly. Joann felt herself again, strong, ready to overcome adversity. The boat straightened, the helm allowed to steer slightly. Jeff smiled at her with satisfaction and as the wind blew her hair, she laughed out loud.

They reached the bay still excited about the adventure and very hungry. The seaside pub was fully packed. An old-looking, iron wood burner smouldered in the corner by the bar, and on the wall was a large helm with colourful pennants hanging above. The warm air smelled of fried fish and cigarette smoke. They ordered fish and chips and beer, sitting facing each other at the end of a long wooden table. The men next to them were fishers and cursed the weather and roped them into a conversation about the vicious robberies of late. Joann noted with relief that she no longer felt the terrifying fear and was more relaxed when talking about it.

"What shall we do with the drunken sailor," someone from the other end of the room sang. A few people joined him in the shanty, and after a while almost everyone was singing loudly and vigorously, stamping their shoes to the beat and hitting the table with fists. It got so loud that Joann and Jeff couldn't hear each other and stopped talking. She stared at him, at his warm, gentle gaze and teasing smile, remembering the last few days they had spent together, and felt a bond between them, and something more than that. She thought bitterly that it would be hard for her if he left back to London.

He took her hand and held it gently as they looked into each other's eyes. The waitress delivered their food, giving Jeff a very provocative look at the same time, and Joann felt a pang of jealousy in her heart. She realised now that she couldn't be happy with Garrett and that what she felt about him was not real.

"I wish I could be with you all the time and never part," Jeff said seriously. "Please tell me what's bothering you, whatever it is. I will do anything to help you." He touched her hand gently. There was a sweet air of deep feeling and Joann felt her heart beating fast.

"You are stealing my heart," she thought. She decided to tell him about her fathers's treasure and Ben's revenge.

It was getting dark by the time they left the pub. It was foggy and impossible to see the sea, although it was only a dozen metres away. One could only hear the waves hitting the shore. Damp and the scent of the sea was in the air. The chill of the evening overwhelmed them. Jeff drove her home. Visibility on the road was poor, but the fog dissipated in the light of the lampposts and headlights. He stopped the car in the driveway and they both got out.

"I don't want you to be alone until they catch those bandits," Jeff said, approaching her.

"I'll be alright," she replied. "Inspector Hawkins says they're probably far away from here now."

"I don't know what I would do if something happened to you," he said. "I think I would die. I will stay here and sleep in the car then."

"But people will gossip."

"Damn it." He opened his hands. "Let's get married then."

"Married?!"

"Yes, today. In this instance," he said loudly and they

laughed together. He came closer to her and said with seriousness, "You know that I'm in love with you, don't you?" He took her face in his hands and looked deeply into her eyes. "And I like this place, the town and the sea, and I know that I would be happy here."

Joann pressed her cheek to his warm hand, closing her eyes for a moment. "What about London?" she whispered. "What would your father say, and Garrett?" She looked at him, waiting for an answer.

"My family would be most pleased and Garrett would be happy for us. You know, he was always caring towards me and my sister. He was the oldest and had a great sense of responsibility. I was the light-hearted one. He built the business and spent his youth working hard, often until late at night. When Meredith left him, he was devastated and we were worried. But now he's met Louise and fell in love again I am hopeful." He stopped and looked gently into her eyes, and she understood what he was trying to say. The caring way he spoke about his brother touched her and all the anger she had towards Louise melted, vanishing forever.

She came closer to him and he took her in his arms and kissed her mouth. His lips were warm and soft and his arms strong and for the first time in a long time she had a feeling of closeness and intimacy. She was bewildered and happy.

They heard an engine and soon a car appeared in the driveway, approaching the house. It was Garrett and Louise. They got out and walked over as the rain started to drizzle again.

"There was another robbery at Broomfield's estate," said

Garrett "Young Broomfield surprised them and was heavily injured."

"My God," Joann said and covered her mouth with her hand.

"That means that the robbers are still here," said Jeff, putting his hands in his pockets and watching Garrett sharply.

"Yes, they are," he said without any doubt. "The inspector thinks you shouldn't stay here tonight, Jo," he looked at her. "It will be better if you spent the night at Louise's. Jeff and I will stay at the hotel and make sure everything is okay there. He has a grudge against you and might want to come back to hurt you, anything can happen, you'd better not be here."

"Please, Jo. I have everything ready for you," said Louise. Joann noticed something warm and friendly in her voice. Louise struck her as a nice person now, and she wondered why she never noticed it before.

"Thank you, Louise," she said.

# *18*

*J*oann, with her dogs, entered Louise's cottage by the small bay. The house was pleasantly warm, and Joann noticed that the iron stove was still smouldering. She was struck by the scent of flowers, light and nice. There was a large bouquet of freshly cut roses on the sideboard and a bouquet of freesias on the table and she guessed that Garrett had brought them. The dogs looked around the room and barked at the patio door until Louise opened it to let them out. Joann was tired but she was too excited about the recent events to go to bed. She sat down in a soft comfortable armchair with a glass of sherry, Louise opposite her on the couch. It was quiet, the fireplace was cracking and the wind was howling in the garden.

"I was wondering," said Joann, "what you have been doing all these years."

"Well, I was trying to live my life." Louise turned her glass of sherry in her hand. "I felt very lonely after Richard and I broke up. I couldn't see him and I knew I couldn't stay here. I decided to go to a big city where nobody knew anything about me and start fresh. I got a job in a restaurant. I met a young barman there, we started dating and soon got married.

Fortunately, he got a small inheritance from a distant relative and I convinced him to open a little coffee shop and sandwich bar. I didn't know anything about running a bar, but I was learning fast."

"Have you been successful?" asked Joann.

"Oh, yes. We had a good location, close to the business centre. Our motto was to serve everything really fresh and we gained a good reputation. We worked really hard and it paid off." She stopped and looked at the large window from which they could hear the rough waves smashing against the rocks somewhere behind the fog. Joann remarked that Louise never mentioned whether she was happy but she didn't dare to ask her. Louise turned her head back to Joann and her eyes followed.

"Our clientele grew quickly. One woman in particular, she came every day and seemed to be fond of my husband. I told him about it and he laughed, assured me that it was nothing to worry about, and I trusted him. When she stopped coming I felt relieved, only to find out later that they were having a secret affair."

"I am sorry to hear that," said Joann.

"I also found out that I didn't love him enough to forgive him and we divorced. He paid me my share of the business. At that time, a man from our town showed up at the cafe. He recognised me and we started talking. He told me that Richard had died two years after I left. I felt guilty that he'd died unhappy and that we could have had at least two more years together, but we didn't. Two dear, priceless years we lost. I decided not to fade any longer around the world and to come back here, to the place I kept the memories deep in my heart, and where I had the most beautiful moments with the man I loved."

The last words were so unexpected that Joann wept quietly, for her brother's image came to her and she saw him and Louise again on the day of their parting. She had to cover her mouth with her hand to hide her emotions. Louise fell silent and seemed absent for a moment, turning the glass in her hand and staring at the golden colour of the drink. The weather worsened drastically. The rain beat against the window panes and the waves roared in the distance. Cool air entered the room through the ajar glass door and filled the space with freshness, bringing the scent of the sea and wet sweet peas and roses from the garden. The room was full of the delicate aroma that had the power to heal troubled souls and calm anxiety. And one could think that it would not be possible to argue in a room filled with it as it would dismantle any disagreement or grudge and turn it into purity.

The phone rang and Louise talked for a while.

"It was Garrett," she said, walking back towards Joann and sitting down on the couch. "Jeff and he will stay at the hotel and will be watching all night."

"My God, I am so afraid of what will happen," Joann said, worrying for Jeff. The thought that something could happen to him was driving her to despair. She had already lost two beloved men, her father and her brother. She realised that maybe because of that she was always afraid to engage in a relationship emotionally, and yet it had happened. She'd fallen in love. She looked at Louise and thought that she must feel the same way about Garrett. She must be scared too. She took two long sips of sherry.

"It's strange that they came here into our town," said Joann, searching for the reasoning, but she was still thinking about Jeff.

"Don't you think it might have something to do with your father?"

"My father? Why do you think so?"

"Your father was doing strange business," said Louise, and it seemed incredible to Joann at first. She wondered how Louise could know such things, but she suddenly remembered that her mother thought the same. "Richard suspected he was buying gemstones and gold from smugglers at low prices," Louise continued. "Apparently he invested all the money from the sale of the store into it and decided to wait until the prices went up for a double profit."

Joann looked at her with tired eyes. It all seemed possible to her now, and she wasn't going to deny it. "So where are all the gemstones and gold then?" she asked.

"Hidden somewhere, I believe."

"There was nothing in the safe," Joann said, shaking her head.

"There wouldn't be anything there. Your father was afraid of a robbery and kept the safe almost empty in case he was forced to open it. He kept all his valuables somewhere else. Richard was looking for it for months. He believed that if he found it, his mother wouldn't force him to marry a daughter of some wealthy friends, and then we could get married. But he never found anything." She looked ahead with sadness.

"Was there no plan or map leading to this hidden place?" Joann asked hoping she knew more.

"There was a plan written on a piece of paper but it

disappeared after your father's accident. Richard said that he always carried it with him in his wallet."

"His wallet was stolen shortly before his accident. One of those bandits stole it. He said he'd been looking for us all these years. Surely because he found the map."

"Why did he search for you now?"

"I don't know. Maybe it was a coincidence. The Greenbergs advertised the hotel in London, maybe he saw it and somehow associated the name."

"It is quite likely."

"He watched our house for several days and said that he wanted to kill me but something scared him and stopped him from doing it." A cold chill ran through her at the memory of these events.

"I have a feeling it was Richard who saved you," Louise said gently.

Joann wasn't sure what to believe anymore. Too much had happened recently and she was confused.

"Next month is the anniversary of his death." Joann looked at her kindly. "Would you go with me to put flowers on his grave?"

"Yes, I would like to," answered Louise.

# *19*

*T*he bedroom in the attic was small but conveniently furnished. It was decorated with ship models, giving it a nautical feel and the sloping roof gave it a cosy character. It was stuffy and she had to open a little window. Joann fell asleep quickly, but she dreamed strange, restless dreams. The dogs seemed to be disturbed too, and moved around the house making noises. After one hour, she woke up chilled.

She remembered the window was open and got up to close it. She looked at her watch; it was only twelve o'clock. Time dragged on relentlessly and she didn't want to go back to bed. She put a dressing gown on and went downstairs. Louise was still there, making tea. It looked like she couldn't sleep too.

"I am dying for a cup of tea," she said. Louise smiled, made her a cup, and set it in front of her.

"I cannot sleep," she said. "I have bad feelings."

"I should be in the hotel with them right now, keeping an eye on everything in case they need help." Joann felt guilty for not insisting she joined them earlier.

"The inspector thought it would be too dangerous for

you," Louise said, clearly trying to reassure her. "Ben wanted to kill you in cold blood and would probably try to do it again if he had another chance."

"I could see the furious hate in his eyes. It was terrifying," said Joann.

"I am glad you came, you are safe here. Inspector thinks they're not looking for small cottages, but big estates. They take money, jewellery and silver."

The phone rang. It was inspector Hawkins wanting to speak to Joann.

"Jo, do you remember if Ben said anything significant or talked about his plans? We are still looking for them," he asked.

"He said he recently repaired a boat, and that he has a sister on the Irish coast. They may try to sail there," Joann tried to be helpful.

"We have all ways to the harbour surrounded. They won't break through. We think they might still be here, somewhere."

"They must have a good hiding place. Inspector," a sudden thought came to her. "There are dungeons under the Castle and a long tunnel that goes across right to the little bay. It was shut years ago but if they found and reopened it...That must be why Ben wanted to stay and work longer in the hotel, because he needed time to open it to have hiding place and escape route."

"Can you take me there?" he said without hesitation.

"Yes. I'll be there in a minute. Louise will drive me."

"Alright, I'll meet you in the Castle. We have no time to waste."

* * *

The downpour made it difficult to see on the slippery road. A strong wind was pushing the small car to the side of the road and Louise drove very slowly. When they reached the Castle it seemed almost deserted. Some of the lights were turned off and there was no one at the reception. They both headed towards the dungeon entrance bumping into Alfred and Piper the night porter.

"Where is Inspector Hawkins?" she asked Alfred.

"He has already gone down to the dungeon with Garrett and Jeff and two policemen. They couldn't wait. They told me to close the entrance so that no one could pass through."

"Open it up. I'm going there," she said determined.

"THIS IS MADNESS," Louise shouted spontaneously.

"I have to help them."

"This is absurd and I can't let you do it," she said nervously trying to stop her. To her she was the litter sister of Richard and now in the face of danger Louise felt strong duty to protect her.

"You can't stop me. Besides, they need a guide. I'm the only one who still remembers these tunnels," she replied firmly.

"You can't go alone," Louise insisted.

"Alfred is going with me," Joann looked at him in the determined manner.

"I knew you would say that," Alfred looked up at the portrait of Sir Roger with anxiety, turn on a flashlight and entered the tunnel.

"Piper, you will lock the door behind us," she said.

"Wait! I am going with you," Louise said in spite of herself, knowing she couldn't do otherwise. Following them she had a bad feeling about it, realising they don't stand a chance against two dangerous criminals. She knew something bad was about to happen. Thinking of death lurking around the corner in the darkness of the corridors, she felt strong will to live. Richard was dead but she wanted to live. She grabbed Joann by the arm tightly touching the stone wall of the narrow corridor with the other hand.

The flashlights were small and the light was short, giving visibility to just a few metres. In the distance ahead was a deep, ominous darkness. They were moving forward quickly and quietly. Joann was thinking soberly now, calculating every move. There was no time for fear and she didn't think about it. She was focused on the clear goal of joining and guiding the chase. She expected the air to be musty here but was surprised to find that it was quite crisp. This meant that the door had to be opened many times recently. This confirmed her belief that the perpetrators were hiding here.

Suddenly from a distance came a barely audible whine, approaching fast and growing lauder. The three of them stopped listening. It was a pitiful howl, full of pain and suffering. It sounded ominous at times and then it was full of sadness again. It was neither a man nor an animal. Only an unknown beast or a tormented soul could make such a horrified sound. It echoed the walls surrounding them on all sides, causing their skin to tingle.

"It's Sir Roger's ghost. He's coming for us," Alfred's voice sounded horrified. Louise's fingers tightened painfully on Joanna's shoulder, but Joann had heard it here before, years ago.

"It's the wind," she whispered. "The door on the other

side must be open."

They came to a fork in the corridor. Joann frowned her forehead concentrating, remembering Richard when he spoke laughing: "As long as you stick to the right side you are safe."

The tunnel on the right was long and led straight into the bay. If the chase with the inspector had gone this way, they would have seen flashlights in the distance, but the tunnel was dark and empty. They must have gone down the other corridor. On the left there was a number of small tunnels, passages and nooks where it was easy to get lost, and a deep cavern.

"This way," she said, turning to the left. She smelled the faint smell of smoke coming from the depths assuring that the chase was headed there by the smell. The only place to light a fire was in the cave. "There must be the hiding place," she thought.

They walked a few metres to the next frank and Joann instinctively headed for the dark passage. A gentle breeze brushed her face and she felt a soft, almost caressing touch on her neck, she shuddered.

"Cobwebs, no one has been here for a long time," she said returning to the next tunnel.

Here the walls were built of timber. The smell of rotten wood was very strong. Some of the torch-lit beams were in disrepair and threatened to collapse at any moment but they paid no attention. They moved slowly, carefully illuminating every nook and cranny, checking if anyone was lurking there in the dark.

They heard the sound of quick footsteps coming from

the opposite direction. Common sense told them to hide. They turned off flashlights, jumping hurriedly into the alleys. Joann pulled terrified Louise behind her and pinned her against the wall. The footsteps came closer, they were heavy and single. "One man," she guessed. It was Ben. He passed them hidden in the dark alley. She could see his back now and held her breath instinctively. His leg was injured and he was clearly limping in a hurry. He stopped unexpectedly. If he turned around he would see them right away. He seemed to inhale air as if intrigued by some strange smell. She thought of the sweet scent of her perfume that must have attracted his attention.

The anticipation of the inevitable confrontation had worn her nerves. She felt faint, ready for the worse. Subconsciously she called for Richard to help her again, thinking to at least save Louise.

Ben hesitated a moment then moved rapidly forward and after a while his footsteps died away in the distance. They waited a while longer before coming out of the hiding. There was no sign of Alfred. He must have jumped into some other tunnel and got lost. Without waiting for him they headed towards the cave. After a dozen or so metres they saw the light and the tunnel went deep down, revealing a large cave with rocky ground and walls. In the middle the fire was slowly burning out.

They noticed a man, it was Jeff, he was alone. He looked around examining some traces, then picked up a small bundle, looked at it and put it in his pocket. The sight of Jeff made Joann happy. He was fine, safe and sand, everything else seemed to her like an unreal farce. She was seized with the illusion that they could simply go home now. At that moment something moved behind him, and the figure of a man emerged from the shadows, arousing tension and fear again. His hand armed with knife rose over Jeff. Joann let out a terrified scream upon hearing this, Jeff turned, but the hand fell down, digging the knife into his flesh. He groaned in pain leaning against the wall. A shot was fired and the assailant fell to the ground. After a few seconds the inspector come running still holding the revolver followed by Garrett and two policemen.

Joann ran down to Jeff clinging to him.

"Jeff," she sobbed.

"It's only the arm," he reassured her.

"The wound is not deep. He will be fine," Hawkins assessed his injury with a practiced eye. "Tie it up," he handed him a handkerchief, then bent over the dead man.

"What are you doing here?" Garrett took Louise by the hand, but she was silent, just looking at him, happy he was alright.

"Where is Ben?" Asked Hawkins.

"He is running away," said Joann. "This way."

They headed back. Jeff was clutching his sore arm. Joann led the way bringing them to the first fork and taking the corridor to the right. It was getting colder as they walk. In the distance, the light of the flashlight revealed the entrance from the bay, it was wide open. The sounds of battle reached them and the policemen rushed forward. Outside two men were fighting with each other.

"Help!" they heard Alfred's familiar voice. He was struggling with Ben who was trying to put his hands around

Alfred's neck. The policemen and Garrett jumped in, quickly pulling Ben away and handcuffed him. Alfred got up slowly from the ground. He was out of breath.

"I followed him but he spotted me and fell on me," he gasped after a while. "He fought like a wild, rabid animal, I thought I was going to die."

When Ben was being taken away, he glanced briefly at Joann and she saw resignation and exhaustion on his face. That was the moment he finally realized he had lost.

The rain's let up a bit but the wind didn't weaken.

"I can't believe he wanted to sail in this weather," said Garrett as he watched the waves toss the little sailboat around in the bay.

\* \* \*

When the four of them got back to Louise's cottage it was still dark, the sky in the east was turning navy blue. After a tiring night, they settled in sofas commenting on past events. There were smiles and relief on their faces.

"Garrett and I looked around the dungeons a bit," said Jeff. "In two places the walls were freshly dug, as if they were looking for something but found nothing. I found a piece of paper that was swept and tucked into the corner. It looks like a dungeon plan and it has your father's name. Could this be the map you were looking for?" He handed her a crumpled piece of paper starring at her lovingly without taking his eyes of her.

Joann had never seen it before. It was very old and

her father's signature in blue ink was faded. There was a sketched castle with dungeons and two supposedly random points placed there. The surrounding buildings were also on the map; her house and garden and the road to the town. She didn't understand what that was supposed to mean. She remembered her father, saw his smiling face with a cunning flash in his eyes. He was a smart man. This plan seemed too obvious and yet it had his signature on it. Maybe it was just a sketch and not a treasure map.

"Father hid precious stones and gold belonging to the family, but we don't know where," she said, still deep in thought.

"Could this be the plan leading to this place?" asked Garrett.

"This is my father's signature," she confirmed.

"There was nothing in the two places marked on it," he continued. "The robbers probably concluded that this map did not indicate anything of value. That's why they decided to rob local houses. Do you see anything special on the map that catches your attention?"

"No, nothing at all," she looked at the map in her hands, still not understanding it. There were no other markings.

"On the other side is the name of a woman," said Jeff, and Joann turned the page over. She could see the name Mary, written twice in her father's hand.

"No, that doesn't tell me anything. See for yourself." She handed the map to Louise. "I think you know more about this than I do."

"Do you not associate this name with anything?" Louise looked carefully at the piece of paper.

"No," said Joann. "I don't know anyone named Mary, and I don't know if my father did." Although now it came to her mind what her mother had said about him having an affair. Was it that woman's name then? The name of his mistress. Did he leave these clues for her and would she know what they meant? Did he really want to leave her all the money? Was it his last will? She wished to be able to answer these questions. It got very quiet. All eyes seemed to be staring at her. The rain stopped and the fog cleared. She could see the light of a lighthouse in the distance on the headland.

"Mary," she said quietly.

"It's not Mary," Louise said, catching her attention. "It says 'Mary, Mary' and three dots. Does that remind you of anything?"

Joann suddenly realised that she actually did associate it with something.

"It reminds me of my father's favourite nursery rhyme. 'Mary, Mary quite contrary'. Even when I was older and walked in the garden with him, he always reminded me that rhyme. But that sounds silly, doesn't it? It definitely has nothing to do with the sketch."

"It's worth checking," said Garrett. "It's the only clue and it sounds quite likely."

"I think the same," added Jeff. "Do you want us to go there in the morning to check it out with you?"

"I would love to," she answered.

They had a hot breakfast and Louise made strong coffee. It was bright outside and the birds chirped. They couldn't wait to go and look for the treasure. They got into the car and soon found themselves on the avenue of chestnut trees. It was cloudy and through the huge branches the sky appeared to be the colour of milk. In the garden, the grass was still wet from the rain. The dogs enjoyed the return home and ran like crazy through the trees, barking. Garrett walked in front carrying a large shovel, Louise next to him, telling him something funny, and they laughed merrily. Jeff put his arm around Joann and hugged her to him. She looked at him happily. Cold raindrops fell from the yew trees as they passed underneath.

"Where to now?" asked Garrett, standing in the middle of the garden.

"Right there." Joann pointed to the boulder near the juniper bush.

The boulder was quite large, wet and slippery. With their joint efforts, they pushed it aside, slipping on the wet grass and having a lot of fun. Garrett rubbed his hands comically, grabbed the shovel and stuck it in the ground. The earth was soft after the rain and he easily dug up the top layer, before hitting something hard. They stopped laughing and immediately became serious, looking at each other with excited eyes and crouching down. They brushed away the rest of the wet, black earth.

There was a metal box in the hole. They all seemed to be holding their breath simultaneously as Jeff took the box in his hands, slowly pulling it out and setting it on the boulder. It was small but quite heavy. The lid was easy to open. He pushed back the black velvet material on top. Coloured cuts of precious stones glistened before their eyes in the daylight.

"My God!" cried Louise.

Joann was moved at the sight of these jewels and tears of happiness filled her eyes. Garrett took a closer look, taking out a handful of small gems.

"Rubies, emeralds and sapphires," he said in an excited voice. "There are also diamonds and gold and silver circlets."

"You found it, Jo," said Louise. "Your father left these clues for you, he knew you would decode them."

"It's your father's treasure," said Garrett. "Now it belongs to you and your mother."

"According to inheritance law," explained Jeff, "half is assigned to his wife and the other half to children."

"I think," said Joann, "that Richard would like Louise to receive his part of the treasure."

Hearing that, Louise started to cry. She covered her face with her hands, sobbing loudly.

# *20*

*I*t was afternoon, the day was grey but windless. Huge dark clouds seemed to hang low. The old cemetery next to the small stone church was empty and still. It was overgrown with tall grass and ivy that crept along the ground and climbed the trees whose sprawling crowns engulfed the daylight. In some places it was dark under their branches and black irises stuck out eerily from the grass. A stone angel with wings covered in green algae and lowered eyelids reminded Joann of the temporal nature of life.

Richard's grave was near the large mahonia bush, overgrown with clusters of dark purple berries. Black morning glory flowers climbed the stone cross and obscured the inscription on the tombstone. Joann walked over and pushed aside the plant's branches, tearing off the dry leaves and faded flowers. Louise lit a candle in a memorial lantern and put it on the tomb. She held a bouquet of roses the colour of a summer sunset. She pressed them to her chest for a moment, then carefully placed them next to the lantern. Joann put a bouquet of white lilies next to it. For a while they stood in silence.

"Rest in peace dear Richard. I will never forget you," said Louise.

"Rest in peace, my beloved brother," said Joann and added after a while, "I think he would be happy to see that we are friends."

"I am sure he is," said Louise.

"Yes, he is happy now." Joann stared at the candle's flame. She felt a slight breeze although the mahonia leaves did not move. It seemed to her that she felt someone's presence in front of her she couldn't touch or see and yet, she was not afraid of it. Suddenly something gently brushed her cheek, like a kiss from someone dear to her. Emotions filled her heart as she put her hand to her cheek, as if she wanted to keep this goodbye kiss. A beam of light broke through the clouds and tree branches, it was blindingly bright, it shone for a fraction of second and then abruptly disappeared. Everything was silent again. Joann looked at Louise, still touched.

"Did you see…?"

"Yes, I did." Louise smiled and put her arm around Joann.

Their hearts were filled with some higher feeling, the feeling of forgiveness and joy. They put more flowers and a candle on her father's grave and said prayers.

"Your father would be proud that you are getting married," Louise said.

"Yes, he would adore Jeff."

An elderly couple came to the cemetery with a bouquet of flowers, passing close by, and Joann wondered what their story was. Her and Louise walked slowly towards the town, both happy and appreciating the value of this feeling. Life had shown them a kind and generous side now, and they were thankful.

"I always wanted us to be a family and for you to be my sister-in-law," said Louise.

"So, it will be. By marrying Garrett, you will become part of our family." Joann looked at her and smiled. "Life writes unbelievable stories."

"It's true," said Louise, "and fate is unpredictable."